Karen grew up in a small town in north-eastern Victoria, Australia where she rode horses through a beautiful landscape of eucalypts, lakes, and snow-capped mountains. Her love of country continues to influence both her fiction and nonfiction writing.

She built a career in a range of educational settings culminating in heading Australia's first writing and publishing degree. She holds a Ph.D. and M.Ed. (Hons) in the areas of myth and fantasy as well as a range of post-graduate qualifications in Education, ESL, and Literacy.

Karen travels extensively overseas but enjoys nothing more than camping in the Australian Outback.

The White Stag and Other Stories with Deep Fantasy Retellings is Karen's first collection of short stories. She is also the author of 17 fantasy novels and three non-fiction books exploring travel, poetry, and Deep Fantasy.

She lives in Melbourne and writes full time. You can find out more about Karen and her books on her website.

Connect with K.S. Nikakis

Amazon: https://www.amazon.com/author/ksnikakis
Twitter: https://twitter.com/KSNikakis
Facebook: www.facebook.com/ksnikakis
Goodreads: www.goodreads.com
Website: www.ksnikakis.com
Email: author@ksnikakis.com

WORKS BY K S NIKAKIS

Non Fiction
Travel and Poetry

Journey: Seeking the Sacred, Spirit and Soul
in the Australian Wilderness
In the Company of Birds: Poems from an
Outback Odyssey
Glastonbury - Meditations on the Goddess

Fantasy Novels
Series

Angel Caste series:
Angel Blood
Angel Breath
Angel Bone
Angel Bound
Angel Blessed
Angel Caste – Complete 5 Book Series

The Kira Chronicles trilogy:*
The Whisper of Leaves
The Song of the Silvercades
The Cry of the Marwing
remnant hard copies only

The Kira Chronicles series:
The Whisper of Leaves
The Silence of Stone
The Secrets of Stars
The Thunder of Hoofs
The Crying of Birds
The Music of Home
The Kira Chronicles – Complete 6 Book Series

Fantasy Novels

The Emerald Serpent
Heart Hunter
The Third Moon
Messenger
I Heard the Wolf Call My Name – *Finalist -*
Best YA Novel Aurealis Awards, 2019
The Dragon of the Drowned World -YA

Fantasy Short Story Collections

The White Stag and Other Stories – With
Deep Fantasy Retellings

THE

WHITE STAG

AND OTHER STORIES WITH DEEP FANTASY RETELLINGS

K.S. NIKAKIS

First published by SOV CONSULTING LLC - SOV Media
Australia 2024 Amazon: www.amazon.com.au

The White Stag, Ghost Stream, Glass-Heart, Rite and Dragon
Sprite were previously published as stand alones on Amazon
KDP

Publisher: SOV CONSULTING LLC - SOV Media Melbourne
Australia

Cover by C. Nikakis
Image: Willy46 Vector 2111104937/Shutterstock.com
Typography: Photoshop/Trajan Color

National Library of Australia
Cataloging-in-Publication entry:
Nikakis, Karen Simpson
The White Stag and Other Stories with Deep Fantasy Retellings
ISBN 978-0-6451927-4-2

Who looks outside, dreams;
who looks inside, awakes.

Carl Jung

Contents

ABOUT DEEP FANTASY

The collection contains a broad range of stories in the Deep Fantasy subgenre. *The White Stag*, *Glass-Heart* and *Dragon Sprite* align with the European fantasy tradition; *Fallen*, *Rite* and *Ghost Stream* draw on Australian Outback settings; and *Werewoman* and *A Prince Lost in a Jungian Dream* are best interpreted in a Jungian context. Unlike the usual short story collection, each story is followed by a Deep Fantasy retelling. So, what exactly is Deep Fantasy? The best way to introduce Deep Fantasy is to consider the story of *Sleeping Beauty* both as an overt, *conscious* story, and as a covert, *unconscious* story, that is, as Deep Fantasy.

In a common version of *Sleeping Beauty*, Aurora (also called Briar Rose) pricks her finger on a spindle on her sixteenth birthday, bleeds, and falls into a very long, magickal sleep to be eventually woken by the kiss of a Prince. We understand this well-known story *consciously* but like so many stories, especially those drawn from myth, nursery tales, and folklore (usually classified as fantasy in the modern era), it provides a *second* story that readers might understand *unconsciously*.

In this second story, Aurora pricks her finger on a spindle and bleeds, that is, begins menstruation. The phallic shape of the spindle also suggests sexual maturity. However, while she has reached physical maturity (in a sexual sense), she has yet to reach psychological maturity and so is removed to a safe place for this to happen. Then, when it has, she is woken (becomes aware of herself as a sexually mature woman) by a male kiss.

The isolation of young women for a period of time (to allow psychological maturity to take place) is also a feature of stories such as *Snow White* (asleep in her glass coffin) and *Rapunzel* (locked away in her stone tower).

This second, covert, deeper story (for which I coined the term Deep Fantasy) works at an unconscious level and is where much of the story's power lies (and the reason for the tale's longevity), even if the reader (and sometimes the writer) isn't *consciously* aware of it.

Deep Fantasy employs a number of literary devices to convey its unconscious meaning including symbolism and metaphor, and often draws on archetypes as well. These devices are common in myth and its close kin fantasy, and more obviously in poetry. They are also common in dreams which is unsurprising given that dreams spring from the unconscious.

While writing (and the production of other artistic artefacts) is a *conscious* activity, one way or another, creative inspiration comes from the *unconscious* and so carries with it a rich range of symbols, metaphors, and archetypes. The writer might use these devices *consciously* to enrich their work (as I do as a Deep Fantasy writer), or use them *unconsciously* and not notice them until the work is finished or perhaps not notice them at all.

For instance, I've not read that Tolkien, in his famous work *The Lord of the Rings*, (consciously) intended the episode of Gandalf's battle with the Balrog in the Mines of Moria, to be other than a hero fighting a demon, but the power of this episode lies in its Deep Fantasy meaning. To descend into the earth (the mines) is to (metaphorically/symbolically) descend into the unconscious, a part of which is the Shadow (discussed in more detail later), which holds the things we dislike, or deny, or fear about ourselves and have banished from our conscious mind.

Gandalf enters the Mines of Moria reluctantly because he senses that death awaits him there, as indeed it does, the death of his old self (also discussed in more detail later).

His battle with the Balrog (a symbol of the things he's banished to his Shadow) is a necessary one for Gandalf (the Grey) to move onto his next life stage as Gandalf the White. No one can simultaneously be a baby and a child, an adolescent and an adult. We must 'die to our old selves' to become our new self. Part of this process is to truly know and accept our present selves in our entirety (warts and all) which means to name, confront, and accept the things in our Shadow (our very own Balrogs).

Ursula Le Guin's fantasy *A Wizard of Earthsea* provides a powerful example of this when, in a fit of pride and arrogance, the young wizard Ged releases a demon into the world. At first the murderous creature pursues Ged but then, as Ged's understanding grows, he pursues it until, in a pivotal scene, he embraces it, and by naming it Ged (his own name but its name too given it's his unpleasant repressed parts) he gains power over it, assimilates it, and so enters his next (better) life stage.

Moving to our next life stage often takes time because confronting and assimilating our Shadow is difficult (which is why so many fantasies contain struggle-filled quests). This place of struggle, between our present life stage and the next, is called the liminal.

Gandalf enters the Mines of Moria as Gandalf the Grey and exits as Gandalf the White, thus the mines serve as a liminal space. The liminal is seen as both tumultuous and dangerous because things are neither one thing nor another, and the 'natural' order of Nature, society, rules of life and death, and so on, lose their power. It's been suggested by some that everything that takes place in Tolkien's *Middle*-earth is in the liminal because it takes place in the period *between* the time of Elves and the time of Men, hence the word *middle* in the name.

Regardless of Tolkien's conscious or unconscious intent, the uncertainty of the liminal is why *mid* anything, such as midnight (neither the last day nor the next) figures so prominently in fairytales such as *Cinderella* and why *mid* summer is central to Shakespeare's *Midsummer Night's Dream*. Crossroads serve the same purpose (a space neither north, south, east or west) which is why they were popular places of execution (the deceased's vengeful spirit was prevented from following the executioners home).

Liminal spaces are often depicted as forests (which separate people from the orderliness of the known world) where strange and 'unnatural' things might dwell. Think *Little Red Riding Hood*, *Snow White and the Seven Dwarves*, and *The Wind in the Willows*, but the liminal can take many forms (such as the isolation of a Covid lockdown).

The key point is that life is about transitions and that the next life stage can't be reached without braving the usually uncomfortable (and sometimes perilous) challenges of the liminal, a journey of transformation carried out in the unconscious. This is the message of countless myths in disparate cultures throughout the ages, and the premise of the famous mythologer Joseph Campbell's equally famous book *The Hero with a Thousand Faces* (discussed in more detail later).

My own journey into the fantasy subgenre of Deep Fantasy was prompted by my master's degree (an examination of the purposes of dragons in literature) which introduced me to the works of Carl Jung and Joseph Campbell, and it was Campbell's universal hero myth that formed the basis of my Ph.D. However, as is often the case, my studies were simply an extension of my natural inclinations. I had long been fascinated by the patterns in my surroundings and my insights into their connection to other (seemingly unrelated) things has grown over time, so that exploring these connections as a writer (especially at an unconscious level) became a natural path to take.

While the following stories were written for many of the reasons writers write: to explore ideas/issues; tell the story hammering away inside my brain; and to entertain, they were mainly written to explore the unconscious journey we all must take through the liminal to our next life stage.

I hope you find both versions of my stories interesting.

THE WHITE STAG

The body was all but hidden in the briars, as if the murderer had tried to ensure the crime remained unnoticed, but the red was shocking against the green, as blood always is. It caught Tom's eye, as did the gleam of bone. His knuckles whitened through his papery skin as he gripped the carved knob of his stick. The knob bore a stag's head, majestic despite the antlers being flattened against its skull. His father's sinewy hand had gripped this knob, and his father's before him, and now the stick helped Tom along in his final days.

The stick should have passed to Alasdair but if things went well, the stick would pass to the Boy. Tom's mouth twisted. It seemed an age since things had gone well.

He dragged in a ragged breath and used the stick to push the thorny canes aside and for a moment simply stared. 'Now there's a thing,' he muttered. He leaned on the stick until he could breathe again and then his gaze searched the surrounding forest. The trees were like a crowd of skeletons with grasping dead fingers that reached out to claim him. He half shook his head. He'd not been given to self-pity and wasn't about to start now.

An abandoned squirrel drey blotched the branches of a nearby ash, stark in winter's thrall, and he started as a black shape broke from the briars and alighted on a branch above his head. 'Away with ye,' he ordered, and brandished his stick. 'I'm not done yet,' he growled. The crow only flew a few branches higher but Tom barely noticed. The stag's head imprinted his palm as he fought to stay upright. 'Ye won't be having me before the hawthorn's a flower,' he muttered, and stumbled away down the slope.

His father's voice echoed in his head to remind him that things must eat to stay amongst the living and you should never begrudged a crow a corpse but Tom lacked the strength to nod his agreement until the path had leveled out.

The air was colder here with a chill that clamped his chest tight but he liked the way the land rose to either side to enclose him even though others shunned this place. Hearn's Track might mark the sign that led away from the village but Tom had always called it Hearn's Holloway like his father. His grandfather had called it Gog's Grundle and there were older, stranger names all but lost in the past.

Whatever it was called, the holloway ran like a decapitated tunnel all the way from the Old Forest's edge to the village outskirts and was dim even in daylight. That and its proximity to St Eustace's graveyard was enough for most villagers to take the smoother, lighter Old Forest Path.

An early mist smudged the way ahead but Tom's thoughts were on his father again and on the grandfather he'd scarcely known. Both men had filled Tom's thoughts of late because Tom yearned to know what they would have done in his predicament but their counsel eluded him, even in dream.

Tom's grip tightened on the stag's head knob again as if the stick that had aided his grandfather and father could aid him too, but his breathing grew so labored he was forced to stop. The mist closed in like a clammy curtain and he licked his cracked lips. It was too soon in the evening for such a mist as it had been too soon in the season for the dead fawn.

Tom's head swam as he feared things slipped out of kilter: a doe that dropped her fawn too early, a winter that lingered far too long, and the young taken before their time. Perhaps the mist was an uncanny thing too, a veil sent to tempt him to the other side to leave the Boy unprotected.

The leafless trees wavered as if seen through water and as pain tore at him like wolves, he fumbled Doc Harris's pills from his pocket. His hands shook and he gagged as he struggled to swallow them but a swig from his hip flask sent them on their way. Despite the Doc's prohibition of alcohol, the whisky was good and there had been scant good things in Tom's life of late.

The beat of pain lessened and he wiped his mouth. Doc Harris might spend his Sundays on bended knee in St Eustace's musty pews but he knew how to kill pain and for that Tom was grateful.

The mist crept closer and Tom raised his stick again, confident now he had its measure. 'Away with ye,' he ordered, as if it were the crow. 'Ye'll not be having me yet!'

The holloway's walls were thick with brambles, the pale roots of ash exhumed by winter storms, and great ropes of ivy that crawled down from the world above. Even when the meadows were alive with light and the Old Forest's new-leafed trees filled with birdsong, the holloway remained dark and silent. And now that mist thickened the air, it was also other-worldly.

Shadows moved ahead and Tom blinked as he heard the measured tramp of feet and saw dim outlines. The shapes were bulky as if the marchers carried packs and there was song too, ebbing and flowing, that roused memories of his grandfather's songs from the Great War.

It was some kind of re-enactment, concluded Tom, annoyed others had invaded the holloway's quiet with their childish games. He slowed to let them draw ahead but they suddenly disappeared leaving the holloway silent again. There was nowhere to hide and Tom had to lean on his stick once more and will himself not to fall. Doc Harris had been right to warn against mixing alcohol with the pills, he conceded, and then forgot about the doctor as something else loomed from the shadows.

Tom blinked hard as a wraith glowed palely where no light shone and his heart pounded as he considered his proximity to the graveyard. And then the wraith was gone.

Pain tore at Tom with renewed ferocity and he washed down more pills with a swig from his flask. 'In for a penny, in for a pound,' he muttered. If he were too weak to resist Harris's pain-numbing pills, he might as well make a decent job of it.

He struggled on knowing Meg would worry if he were late and, after a while, the holloway slowly rose to join the land above. The incline was gentle but enough to make him wheeze and then he was back on the Old Forest Path, his gaze on the yellow glow in the distance. Meg would be in the kitchen making jams and marmalades from expensive store-bought fruits. As if she could bottle up all that was good in the world and keep it safe! 'Nothing's safe, Meggy,' he mumbled, exhaustion slurring his words. 'Nothing's ever safe.'

He was glad his cottage was close to the Old Forest and several hundred yards from its neighbours. He didn't want their pots of stew left warm on the doorstep or their pity; he wanted things back the way they were before, with three chairs at the table instead of two. His hand trembled as he opened the back door, but he managed to hang up his coat and stow his stick without faltering, knowing Meg watched him.

She stood in the kitchen doorway, the light behind transforming her wild red curls into a halo. The jam smelled of summer and he drew a deep breath knowing there would be no more summers for him.

'You're late,' she said, as she wiped her hands on her apron. It was neither an accusation nor a nag but fear that another of them had been taken. Alasdair's pet name for Meg had been Angel but when Tom had first met her, he'd thought her too homely for the name. Yet Meg had anchored Alasdair and kept him safe, at least for a little while, and now she kept what was left of Alasdair safe too, so Angel she was. 'You've seen Dr Harris?' she asked, as Tom washed his hands at the sink.

'That I have.'

'And what did he say?' She called the question over her shoulder, busy at the stove, the ladle chinking on the bowls as she served the soup. She set the bowls on the small wooden table and sat, her apron pushing up over her belly. Tom stared at the soup as he fought the urge to reach over to reassure himself the Boy was well.

'You know there's nothing left to say, Meg,' he said gruffly, taking up his spoon.

'But the pain. Did he give you something for the pain?'

'He gave me pills,' he said. In truth, Harris had prescribed the pills weeks ago and on this visit had upbraided Tom for not taking them. 'Seem to work,' he added, and took several slurps of soup. The chemo had robbed him of taste but he ate to please Meg and to shore up his chances of seeing the Boy. 'And you?' he asked, looking up at her. 'Are you well?'

She nodded and he resisted the urge to badger her. The rules of the small cottage were unspoken but clear: a couple of questions each, to be answered honestly, no matter how bad the news. Tom guessed some sort of pact had existed between Alasdair and Meg too, though it wasn't his place to ask. Whatever it was had calmed Alasdair's wild ways enough for him to create something rather than just thoughtlessly destroy.

Tom had never seen his restless son truly happy until Meg had appeared but then Tom had moved back into the cottage. Just for a few months, he'd promised, when Meg had insisted he return to the small wooden house he'd passed onto them. Old Harris might be a God-botherer, but he knew his stuff, and the cancer had unfolded pretty much as the Doc had described. But Tom had wondered, in the bitter small hours when the wolf-jaws of pain were at their most ravenous, whether his return had cursed his son.

The Doc might have faith in threesomes: the Father, Son and the Holy Ghost, but watch any group of kids at play, and three was the Devil's number, with two ganging up against the third. Not that he'd ever felt anything but loved and welcomed. He'd raised Alasdair in the cottage and it had been a happy place, as it had for Alasdair and Meg until the truck driver who'd stayed too long at the Hunt and Hounds had met Alasdair's motorbike going too fast near the holloway, and now there were just the two of them again, and the Boy.

Meg found escape in her making, so that the kitchen shelves were lined with jars of jams and marmalades, their deep crimsons and bright citrus colours preserved forever behind clear glass, and she sought solace in the dim spaces of St Eustace's too, as Doc Harris did. Tom had no interest in such consolations but he'd reached the point where he must swallow the Doc's pills or inflict his pain on Meg, and Meg had enough of her own to bear.

Tom spent his days walking the crisscrossed tracks of the Old Forest, the trees as much a sanctuary for him as St Eustace's was for Meg, but the forest's chill shafts of light were far more brutal than the muted blues and golds of St Eustace's stained glass. There was no pretense in a winter forest, no sentiment in a fawn destined to be crow-food, and no comfort in the empty darkness of the holloway, except that last night it hadn't been empty.

Tom had decided, in the sleepless hours of the night, that pain, whisky, and Doc Harris's magic pills provided explanation enough for what he'd seen or thought he'd seen, and he'd sworn to take no more pills, but as the day wore on and pain clawed at the very heart of him, his hand strayed to the packet in his pocket.

The wind was bitter before the spire of St Eustace's loomed in the distance, garlanded with its graveyard of bone-pale crosses, and Tom was grateful to scramble down into the shelter of the holloway. Its banks were steep here and he took the skin from his hands as he gripped some ivy to stop himself falling. The effort cost him dearly and he remained bent as he tore pills from the pack and washed them down with whisky.

It was a while before he managed to get air into his lungs but then they emptied again. A white stag stood less than twenty paces off, its luminous eyes fixed on him, its antlers like the moon-washed branches of a tree. 'Now there's a thing,' he whispered, then the bell at St Eustace's tolled, a crow broke cover, and the stag was gone.

\Tom slumped against the bank. He'd walked the Old Forest countless times during his life and most days over the last few months, and had seen no white fawn or buck, and yet this stag held the majesty of maturity. Then he realised he had seen it before, last night, wraith-like, after the pills and whisky had addled him enough to conjure the soldiers.

His heart faltered as he wondered whether the soldiers had been real too but then he dismissed the idea. A stag, even a white one, was a natural part of the Old Forest, whereas soldiers from the Great War were not, and yet it troubled him that a fully-grown stag should appear from nowhere.

He wondered suddenly if it heralded his death. White animals were always special, mystical even, and as shock at the possibility rolled over him, he swayed, grabbed at the ivy, and missed. He had no sense of falling or of hitting the ground, or of how long he lay there but it was the cold that roused him. He was so numb it took him an age to struggle to his knees. His stick was lost in the darkness and he groped around and shut his eyes in relief when he found it.

It was completely dark and Meg would be worrying. He swallowed two more pills, took a swig of whisky, and set off as fast as his legs would carry him but had not gone far before he heard marching. It came from behind him and anger rose like gorge in his throat as he suspected a group of yobs were having some fun at his expense. Well, they were in for a surprise. He turned and raised his stick, determined at least one of them would go home with a sore head.

The night was clear and while the sound of marching drew closer, no one appeared. His heart thudded but he stood his ground. 'Show ye selves,' he growled, and tightened his grip on the stick. The air moved around him and he saw the shine of helmets crested with crimson, smelled leather, and heard the chatter of a strange tongue, and then there was nothing.

He was proud of having stayed upright but not of the sour stream of bile that erupted from his throat. He leaned on his stick until he was done then wiped his mouth on his kerchief. 'A lesson to ye, Tommy, not to mix ye pills with booze,' he muttered. 'They don't just mess with ye head but with ye belly too.'

Meg waited for him at the cottage door, arms folded across her chest in annoyance or against the cold. A bit of each, he concluded. 'I was thinking of looking for you, Pa,' she said, taking his arm and helping him in. 'Why, you're frozen. To the fire with you.' Tom would have liked to shrug her off but it was hard even to stand and Meggy meant well. 'Where have you been?' she demanded.

She had him in the chair now next to the fire and was busy stoking it. Her curls glinted in its blaze like the helmets he'd glimpsed and understanding dawned. 'Romans,' he muttered. 'Bloody Romans.'

'What?' she asked, turning to look at him but he shook his head. 'You sit there while I fetch you some soup,' she ordered. 'And don't move.'

Meg really was annoyed and Tom felt an odd mixture of irritation and shame. He neither wanted her fussing nor needed it. Doc Harris should have warned him the pills played mind-games and he wondered what other special effects were in store.

Meg came back with a bowl of soup and set it on the side table. 'Warm now?' she asked.

Tom nodded and let Meg ease him out of his coat. She took it, his gloves, and his stick back to their rightful place near the back door then settled beside him. Her blue eyes were expectant but Tom picked up the spoon and began to eat.

'I've been thinking,' she said after a little. Tom's hand tightened on the spoon; thinking wasn't part of the pact. 'It's been three months, Pa. I want you to visit Alasdair with me.'

Tom shook his head. He hadn't attended the funeral because Meg wanted it in St Eustace's and Alasdair's body in the ground afterwards, and it had been her right to choose. Had it been left to Tom, Alasdair's ashes would have joined his forebears' scattered throughout the Old Forest, where Tom's ashes would soon lie. The men of his family were woodsmen, or gamekeepers, or foresters; folk who saw the glory of the sun's rise and set amongst the trees; the uncurling of new bracken and its blackening by frost; the mighty oaks felled by storms to be reborn as green-leaved acorns; the hide, and hair, and bones of dead creatures, shot through with the bright caps of mushrooms.

A church was a small, crouched thing by comparison, its spire puny, its graveyard a prison for those who should be free. Alasdair's grave was marked with a stone cross; he knew that much because Meg had told him, but he hadn't seen it and nor did he want to. Alasdair had loved his freedom in life and it was wrong to confine him in death, but Tom said none of these things to Meg. She acted out of love and he had no argument with that.

Meg still waited and Tom swallowed down the last spoonful of soup. 'Ye know my feelings about churches, Meggy.'

'You don't need to come into the church, Pa, just to the graveyard.' Tom shook his head, his eyes on his empty bowl and felt Meg's warm hand grip his. 'I need you, Pa.' The words were a knife in his heart and he looked up. This was not part of the pact either! Her eyes were full of the tears he hadn't seen since that dreadful night but he knew she'd shed many since, as he had, in the quiet darkness of his room.

'When?' he asked, ashamed to have lost track of his son's death.

'This Sunday, after the service. It will be three months,' she repeated.

Tom nodded, though every shred of his being rebelled. 'Just the churchyard, mind,' he said gruffly. 'And just for a moment.'

Her grip tightened on his hand then withdrew, leaving him bereft. 'Thank you, Pa,' she said.

Tom regretted his pledge as soon as he'd made it and over the following days considered ways to wriggle out of it. But it was pointless. He'd said yes to Meg and that was that. He'd only promised a brief visit, he consoled himself, as he trudged the Old Forest's tracks, careful to take those well shy of the church.

By Saturday he was down to the last of Harris's pills and knew he must visit the Doc for more. It was no use pretending he could get through the days without them; he just hoped they'd be enough for him to meet the Boy. As Meg watched him fumble on his coat that morning, she suggested for the first time he stay at the cottage and rest.

'I need to walk, Meggy.'

'I know, Pa,' she said, fixing the rest of his buttons for him and picking up his stick. 'Alasdair loved stags too,' she said softly, as her fingers traced the knob. 'The only thing in the forest truly free, he used to say.' She smiled a smile that failed to reach her eyes. 'He was wrong,' she added. 'Crows are free. Don't give a damn about anyone or anything.' She smiled again and this time her eyes lit too.

'But not as handsome as stags,' said Tom dryly. His voice was croaky now as if the cancer had reached his throat. If it had, he didn't want to know. His pace had slowed as well but he was in no rush. All he wanted was to live long enough to see the Boy.

He was aware of Meg's gaze on him as he walked away but didn't look back. Alasdair was dead and he was dying. Soon there'd only be Meg and the Boy. She knew it and so did he and that none of it could be undone.

The hawthorn buds were still as hard as gravel and coated with a hoarfrost to form a colder and bleaker type of blossom. His breath plumed in short, sharp puffs like a runner's but all he could do was totter, so unsteady he feared his neighbours believed he spent his days at the Hunt and Hounds.

He turned down into the Holloway, relieved to walk unseen and set off towards the village. His father said the holloway had been carved out over hundreds of years by countless feet, beasts of burden, and wagons, and that if the

11

stone were harder, there'd be no sign of those who'd passed that way.

Tom took a harsh breath. It seemed important suddenly, that there was a sign of Alasdair's passing, and of his own, and that the two of them didn't simply follow all the other nameless travellers into oblivion. He wiped his shaking hand across his mouth and felt the temperature drop. Colder air settled in the holloway's depths but this was something different and he sensed the start of another mind-tricking episode.

There was certainly nothing natural about the mist that swirled about him or the visitors it brought. At first Tom thought the figure he saw was a poacher with an ill-gotten pheasant slung about his shoulders but then realised it was the hindmost walker in a line of other walkers. They were skin-clad, their naked backs and legs pale in the silvery light. The men carried packs and spears, the women hide-wrapped bundles or small children. They went without speaking and then they were gone.

'You need to have a chat to Doc Harris about these visitations, Tommy,' he muttered, but knew he wouldn't give the Doc any excuse to take the pills away or cart him off to somewhere safer. Harris had mentioned the local hospital more than once or having a nurse visit the cottage to ensure he was as comfortable as possible. Tom snorted. They both knew there was no comfort in death!

He swallowed the last of the pills and followed them with a generous gulp of whisky then leaned back against the bank and closed his eyes. The temptation to give up and die was overwhelming but he forced his eyes open again and there it was, the white stag, standing right in front of him.

It was closer this time, its coat aglitter with water droplets, its magnificent antlers snow-bright against the tangled branches. Tom stared at it hungrily, and the strange thought came to him that if it were Death, he would go with it willingly, but then a dog barked somewhere in the village, and the stag sprang away.

Tom struggled after it, wonder displacing pain, and for the first time in months, felt a flicker of hope. He was sure the stag was real although a part of him knew it might be as amorphous as the other pill and booze-fueled apparitions. Soldiers from the Great War, then those from Rome, and now some sort of Iron Age tribe. It was as if the holloway took him backwards in time or else brought these others forward, or maybe the holloway showed him that time didn't matter and that all human journeys were the same.

Tom grunted in disgust. 'Whisky and pills, Tommy, and a cancer that's likely eating away at ye brain. Don't look for explanations where there are none. Just keep on going, one foot after the other, until the Boy arrives. Then you can rest.'

He was almost to the village when he heard the commotion. Car horns and sirens, and someone on a loudspeaker. He struggled out of the holloway surprised to see that police cars blocked the way.

He tottered forward to be met with a firm hand on his chest. 'No further, sir,' said a young constable Tom didn't recognise. 'There's a stag loose in the village. Seems to have wandered in from the forest. We're trying to tranquilize it but if all else fails, it will have to be euthanized. Can't have the public risked.'

'A stag?' croaked Tom.

'Yes, sir, a white one. Wandered in from—'

Tom pushed past him and forced his failing legs into a staggering run. He needed to get to the stag before the police did. He needed to . . . Then a single gunshot reverberated though the silence in his head and he was falling.

He woke in his bed in the cottage although it took him a while to work out where he was. Meg sat propped in a chair beside him, her hands clasped over her belly. 'Doctor Harris wanted you in the hospital but I said you had to be here,' she said, without preliminaries. 'Just as well you signed those papers to put me in charge.' She looked uncharacteristically stern and Tom held his tongue. 'Of course, Dr Harris is right. You should be in the hospital.'

Her gaze on him was unwavering and he moistened his lips. 'I want to be here,' he croaked.

'I know, which is why you are.' She paused. 'You like your freedoms just like Alasdair did. The freedom to live and the freedom to die.'

'Meggy ...'

She rose and smoothed down her apron. 'Don't forget St Eustace's tomorrow. The service ends at three. I'll meet you at the graveyard gate.'

Tom gave himself plenty of time to reach the graveyard. Doc Harris had left him a new supply of pills which helped and Tom had replenished his whisky flask which also helped. He took the Old Forest Path where the light was brighter and where shafts of weak sunshine penetrated the iron-grey clouds.

The service was still in progress when he arrived and he propped himself against the graveyard wall to the far side of the church door. The wall was as grey as the sky but softened here and there with emerald moss. He kept his gaze on the church door to avoid looking at the graves behind him and saw the door open and those inside emerge. Meg was easy to pick, her red curls bright against her blue coat as she paused to talk to others, nodded her goodbyes, and made her way over to him.

14

He hoped suddenly there would be someone else for her one day; someone to love her and the Boy; someone to heal her pain. The idea surprised him and he was ashamed it hadn't come to him earlier.

'I'm glad you're here, Pa,' she said, looping her arm through his and leading him towards the gate.

Tom couldn't say the same but he was glad of her company and of her warm arm keeping him steady. She led him on past graves so aged their inscriptions had been lost, to where the ground was higher. Alasdair's grave faced the Old Forest rather than east as most of the graves did, and because of its elevation, winter blackened trees were visible above the wall.

She brought Tom around to the front of the grave and her grip tightened as he swayed. Birth date, death date, beloved son of, beloved husband of . . . Tom stopped, his gaze fixed on the graven image set right in the middle of the cross.

'A stag,' he choked. 'Why, Meggy?'

'Because we both loved Alasdair.' Tom stared at her in confusion. 'Do you know the story of Saint Eustace, Pa?' Tom shook his head. 'He was a Roman soldier who saw the crucifix in the antlers of a stag he was about to kill, didn't kill it, and converted to Christianity.'

'The police killed the white stag,' said Tom thickly.

'I know, the congregation were furious. It took Father MacGregor most of his sermon to calm us down.' She paused. 'But what Father MacGregor said about hope is true. Saint Eustace was killed and Christ crucified, but not hope. Hope never dies. Christ rose again and there will be other stags, even white ones, to remind us of the fact.'

She regarded him steadily. 'But as a woodsman, you already knew that, didn't you, Pa? That death is matched by new life. It was Christ's message too and perhaps the stag's that Saint Eustace saw.'

There was a long silence. 'I might rest here a little while, Meggy,' said Tom eventually, his gaze on the stag.

Meg patted his arm. 'There's a seat over there that gives a good view of the grave and of the Old Forest. I sit there often. Just me, and Alasdair, and the Boy, but I'm glad you're here now too, Pa.'

Tom's breath escaped in a long, slow sigh. 'So am I, Meggy,' he said softly. 'So am I.'

The White Stag Deep Fantasy Retelling

I spend a lot of time (with my husband) travelling in the Australian Outback, lands loosely defined as those encountered when you leave Australia's coastal fringes behind and head inwards. Australia's heart is sparsely populated, arid, and home to wonderful blood-red and sage-green landscapes, superb 360 degree views of sunrises and sunsets, and the most star-dense night skies you're likely to see anywhere in the world.

It was on one such trip in 2021, having escaped Victoria when its border briefly opened (the Covid lockdowns closed the borders of Australia's southern states as well as Australia's international borders) that I happened to see an article about the death of a white stag in the UK.

It caught my attention because white creatures of any species (not normally white) take on a special significance mostly aligned with the sacred (although there are cultures where it's dangerous or even deadly to be born with Albinism).

White crows, white whale calves, white snakes all regularly make the news, and so it was with the white stag, although the interest was intensified by the stag having been shot dead by the local police and by the outrage that had followed its death. Despite Australia's large feral deer population, a white stag anchored the story in the European fantasy tradition of dark forests and holloways (a landscape feature that's long fascinated me for reasons detailed later).

The death of the stag, an animal often associated with the sacred, suggested a story about one of life's major transitions, that from life to death. *In The White Stag* Tom accepts he is dying, so his transition isn't one of acceptance of death but about moving from a place of despair to one of hope, and the holloway, because of its nature, is an obvious liminal space for this transition to occur.

A holloway is a deeply indented pathway/trackway formed by many generations of people/carts/animals travelling the same route over soft stone. As such, it is both made by time and because of its origins, in a sense, timeless. And so it is here, in the holloway, where the normal workings of time are suspended, that Tom first sees soldiers of the Great War, then Roman soldiers, and lastly Iron Age people. In being taken back in time, Tom is situated in his own life journey which, like the life journeys of those who have gone before him, is one from birth to death (and whatever lies before birth and after death). He becomes one of a community (of humanity) rather than an individual who struggles on alone.

The holloway is also where he sees the white stag, a creature he recognises the sacred in and one that inhabits both the liminal world of the holloway and the normal world above. Until the white stag's appearance, Tom is driven only by a stoic determination to live long enough to meet his unborn grandson. His life consists of an endless walking of barren winter forests (symbolic of his lifeless state) and he lacks even the ability to offer consolation to his bereaved daughter-in-law and to receive it in turn.

The white stag breaks this cycle because, despite Tom's failing strength, he runs from the holloway (back into the 'real' world and connection) in an attempt to save it and, despite his antipathy to religion, visits his son's grave in the churchyard for the first time to provide comfort to his daughter-in-law and in doing so, find comfort himself.

It is here in the churchyard back in the 'real' world, after the transitional change wrought by the white stag in the holloway's liminal, that he understands the wonders of the forest (he's familiar with as a woodsman) and the wonders religion preaches, are not mutually exclusive, but rather parts of the same thing. They are the cross the Roman martyr Eustace saw in the antlers of a deer, a point emphasised by the stag engraved on the cross of his son's grave. And as other elements in the story suggest (watery sunshine breaking through the winter clouds, emerald moss on the stone wall, his sudden wish for his daughter-in-law to find love and happiness once more) Tom's new self is able to experience hope/acceptance/peace in the world again.

DRAGON SPRITE

'Dragon sprites,' hissed Lyt, voice tight with excitement.

'False-sprites,' countered Genn, arching her back in the dapple of warm sunshine she'd claimed on the bough below. She tucked her hands behind her head and serenely gazed up at the leaves' dance of sunlight and shadow.

'How do you know?' demanded Lyt, peering down. 'You can't even see them from there.'

'What season is it?' asked Genn.

'White,' said Lyt, in a small voice.

'I don't need to see,' said Genn, and stretched languidly. She extended her claws and climbed the aisht trunk to the branch Lyt occupied. Her claws pierced the bark and she licked them clean, enjoying the sap's sticky sweetness. 'You *do* have a good view,' she said, settling on her haunches and peering out over Arborin's canopy.

'Not of dragon sprites,' said Lyt morosely, and squinted up at the flight of emerald shapes, dark against the sky's blue.

'They're easy to confuse,' acknowledged Genn and, with lightning reflexes, snatched one from the air. Her claws formed a cage so as not to damage the false-sprite's papery wings but its snout squirted smoke in displeasure. Genn was in no danger of being scorched, given the false-sprite was too young to produce fire, and she held it up for Lyt to see.

'False-sprites have scales of solid green,' she said, and smiled as its red eyes glowered at her. 'If this were a dragon sprite, its scales would shift between gold, bronze *and* green, *and* it would flame me.'

'Even though it's so small?' asked Lyt, eyes grey with wonder.

'Best not to mistake size with power like the Waiwin do,' said Genn dryly. 'And in their case, the larger they are, the more foolish.' She opened her hand but the false-sprite continued to glare. 'You're free to go, *would-be* dragon's spawn,' she admonished. 'Fly!' She tossed it into the air and watched it flap away.

'I yearn to see a *real* dragon sprite,' sighed Lyt.

'Believe me, you don't,' said Genn.

'But they're small. What harm could they do?'

Genn stared at the younger Velven sternly. 'Have you heard *nothing* I've said?'

'I've heard everything but still I yearn,' said Lyt.

'All Velven yearn,' said Genn rising. She unfurled her wings and extended their aqua wing-tendrils. 'I might—' she began, and ducked as something all but clipped the branch beside her head. 'Stink-beetles!'

'No, Orin,' said Lyt, her wide-eyed gaze on the Waiwin who executed perfect aerobatics in the sky above. 'He's still courting you, I see.'

'He can court a false-sprite for all I care.'

'He flies well,' teased Lyt.

'So does a crow.'

'Ah, but a crow's wings don't flash crimson like Orin's do.'

'No, but its brain works and I find a working-brain a very beautiful thing.'

'And I find a muscular chest a very beautiful thing,' said Lyt, and sighed again.

'You'll grow out of it,' said Genn.

'Why won't you *accept* him?' asked Lyt curiously. 'He's the most wondrous of the Waiwin.'

'And knows it.'

'And the fastest.'

'And knows it.'

'There are many Velven who'd gladly *accept* him even when white-eyed,' persisted Lyt.

'And he knows that too,' snapped Genn, and then softened her voice. 'What you'll learn, my sweet young Velven, is that the desire of a Waiwin like Orin is fed by things he *cannot* have. He pursues me, not because I'm beautiful, or fast, or smart, although I'm all these things, but because I won't *accept* him. I am a challenge, my darling Lyt. Were I to lock wings with him, he'd be gone in a flash.'

'Maybe if you *did* lock wings with him, he'd cease bothering you,' suggested Lyt tentatively.

'Ah, but where would be the fun in that? The fast, handsome, *strong* Orin would be at peace, but he'd also be smug and a smug Waiwin is the worst kind of Waiwin of all.' Genn's eyes darkened. 'Besides, Orin's no nester. I want a true-lock, Lyt, so when I raise my young, it won't be on my own.' Genn's eyes greyed again and she brought a wing-tendril gently down Lyt's face. 'Let me know if you see any more *dragon sprites*, sweetling,' she said, and sprang from the branch.

Genn flew straight up and not just because she enjoyed seeing the limitless blue sky above her. A Waiwin's wing shape made it hard for them to fly vertically. Orin didn't try but swept in circles around her instead to gain height in an ever-narrowing spiral. It was a clever strategy and one Genn didn't believe he'd thought of in the instant she'd left the trees. He'd obviously studied her tactics and developed a plan to counter them *or so he thought.*

Genn waited until Orin's spiral reached *axeel*, the minimum distance a Waiwin can approach a Velven who *hasn't accepted him*, and then swerved towards him to narrow the gap. Orin's eyes flashed to black in shock but before he could respond, she folded her wings and dropped.

The strength that drove Orin's pursuit had surged to his wing-tendrils in readiness for locking and he'd struggle even to stay aloft until it flowed back. Genn grinned and her grin broadened as she plummeted towards the trees, spread her wings, and sped off just above their crowns.

Aisht, fyr, beam, zlat: Arborin's trees flashed past, clad in their White Season foliage. The Rimming Peaks were white too and the ice that puddled the Broken Vales, but springs still bubbled in ferny rivens, and she turned towards a riven she'd visited many times.

A quick glance over her shoulder confirmed the sky was empty of Orin and she extended her claws, vanned her wings to slow, and snagged a zlat crown. The zlat were thick here and left little space to land and as the branch bent under her weight, she was showered with blossom.

Zlat were the only Arborin tree to bloom in White Season but their tangy blossoms attracted flintsaurs and Genn opened her mouth to search for their scent before she descended. Flintsaur scent was there as usual but not close and she set off over the emerald moss.

Genn left no print but saw indentations where crystal-flames had lounged and rucked lines where lace adders had hunted them. The riven narrowed and the trees gave way to the first tumbles of glass-stones. Most rivens held glass-stones but the glass-stones here were so pure they looked like giant dew drops.

Genn had visited as a young Velven to admire the slant of her eyes and the fall of her violet hair in their shining mirror surfaces, but lately she had come to admire their perfect egg-shapes. She smiled as she went on up the riven, looking forward to seeing the glass-stones in the shallow bowl of land at the end.

There the breeze trapped Zlat blossom to form a soft grey circular sea with the glass-stones sitting like shining islands in the middled. There was a cavern at the back but the glass-stones took all Genn's attention and she had never bothered to explore it.

The riven twisted before it broadened and Genn's eyes darkened in shock. Every glass-stone had been smashed, their shining remnants spread far and wide, and there was no mystery as to the culprit. A great she-dragon lay amidst the wreckage, or at least, the remains of a great she-dragon.

The flintsaurs had been busy, Genn saw in disgust, and stilled as their pungent scent thickened. Flintsaurs were drawn by movement and the feasting that had reduced the she-dragon to a pile of broken scales and gnawed bones meant dozens of flintsaurs might still lurk nearby. Genn hoped they were well and truly sated but she didn't want to find out. Flintsaurs might be wingless but their muscular haunches gave them a leap that plucked crows from the sky.

Genn's eyes greyed again as curiosity replaced fear. Dragons didn't frequent Arborin in White Season but something had brought the she-dragon here and Genn's gaze reluctantly went to the cavern. The dragon's bones were scored where saber-sharp teeth had raked them and splintered where powerful jaws had searched for marrow, but flintsaurs had no interest in dragon scales. They lay in untidy heaps, grey, dull brown, and rusty-red like the brittle leaves of Fall Season.

There were no emerald-colored scales which told Genn the dragon had been old. Perhaps it had sought out the cavern to die, as dragons sometimes did, and its strength failed before it reached the cavern's shelter.

Flintsaurs were no threat to a dragon in the full-flame of health but an ailing, frail dragon might fall victim to them. But there was another reason why a she-dragon might seek a cavern, even a she-dragon whose scales bore the colours of death, and that was to lay one final clutch of eggs.

Genn's eyes darkened as she surveyed the shattered glass-stones. Their loss saddened her but her gaze didn't search for glass-stones that had somehow escaped the destruction, but smaller, opaque objects of a similar shape.

She found the first fragments of eggshell at the cavern's entrance, as clean as the Rimming Peak's snows, and followed their trail deeper into the cavern's dimness. Dragon sprites took nourishment from the yolk inside their shells, right up to when they used snout-spikes to hammer themselves free, but there were no neat holes in these shells, nor yolk-smears. These shells had been crushed, their dragon sprites torn out, and all traces of life licked clean. Sadness surged again, so powerful her wing-tendrils dulled to powder-blue. The she-dragon had used her dwindling strength to birth one last brood but to no avail.

Genn went on, hardly knowing why she followed the grim trail of shattered eggs given the risk of flintsaurs emerging from their hiding places but, just as she was about to turn back, she glimpsed a pale unbroken curve wedged behind fallen stones.

She extended her claws and carefully eased the egg out, even as she told herself its underside would be crushed but it was intact and she closed her eyes in relief as she cradled it. A flutter within the egg betrayed a pulse but as she considered how close it might be to hatching and the danger of being flamed, something scraped behind her. Stink-beetles! She clutched the egg close and clamped her wings tight over it for extra protection. Every instinct demanded she take to the air and if worse came to worse, relinquish the egg to the flintsaurs to escape, but even the *idea* of killing the dragon sprite made her wing-tendrils curl.

'Coming here was a terrible decision even by your standards, Genn.'

Bless the Seasons! It was Orin. She was so relieved she actually smiled at him but fortunately the cavern's gloom hid it.

'Don't you realise how dangerous it is?' he demanded, his dark outline drawing closer.

'Of course I do,' she said, and snapped her mouth shut as his heady fragrance invaded her senses.

'There are at least twenty flintsaurs between us and the cavern's entrance and probably more by now. Your foolishness has trapped us both.'

'I'm only taking credit for my foolishness,' she retorted. 'You didn't have to come.'

'You know why I came,' he said, stopping less than a wing-breadth away.

'You break axeel,' she warned.

'No, I don't. You accepted me.'

'If you believe that, you're more of a fool than I thought!'

'I hardly think that's possible,' he muttered, but stepped back. 'Why come here anyway? There's nothing to be found but the stench of a dead dragon and its smashed eggs. The flintsaurs are so bloated they won't need to feed till next White Season although I'm sure they'll make an exception for a tasty Velven or Waiwin.'

'Not all the eggs were smashed,' said Genn, and unfurled her wings.

'That's a perilous thing, Genn!' cried Orin in alarm. 'It would've been better left with its kin.'

'To be eaten by flintsaurs? Your idea of *better* is obviously different to mine.' She brought her wings around it again but Orin was right. A dragon sprite was savage from the moment it burst from its shell. At best it would see her as a threat, at worst, as its first meal, but she refused to abandon it. 'The egg stays with me,' she said.

And we stay trapped until the flintsaurs come looking,' grunted Orin.

'You can stay *trapped* if you want, I'm certainly not!'

Orin's crimson wing-tendrils flared. 'You're not going to try to fly out, are you?'

Orin probably feared having to call on his Waiwin honour to protect her. 'You confuse my foolishness with yours,' she said tartly. 'I'm going to use a different exit.'

'You know of one?'

'No yet.'

'Surely you're not going even deeper into this stinking black maze?'

'Given the choice between being a flintsaur snack or enjoying your company, the stinking black maze looks good!'

Genn braced for his retort but he said nothing and as the silence stretched, she felt shamed by her outburst. 'Do you have a better idea?' she asked.

'I'm too foolish.'

His anger was almost as strong as the dragon's stench and she pressed her lips together and set off into the gloom. He kept pace at the precise distance axeel demanded and, along with his continued silence, it added to her irritation. 'Have you been to this riven before?' she asked finally.

'Many times to the riven, never to this cavern.'

Genn looked at him in surprise. 'I've never seen you here.'

'That's because I didn't intend you to see me.'

'You spied on me?' she accused.

'If I spied on anything, it was on what drew you here, so I could learn more of you.'

'Why bother learning more of me?' It was easier to talk to Orin when the darkness hid his face although it didn't hide his wing-tendrils and their brightness told her he was still angry.

'Why do you think?'

Because you're a nosey, vain, smug Waiwin? But she didn't say it, reluctant to add to the ill will between them. She shrugged. 'I don't know. You tell me.'

'Ah, at last something the beautiful axeel-breaching Velven doesn't know. Think about it, Genn.'

'I have,' she said, riled again. 'You want to know everything about every Velven because as a smug, self-important Waiwin, you think it's your right.'

'Wrong,' he said equably.

'Because this riven's a special place I go to avoid you, and you want to make sure I don't avoid you?' she asked sarcastically.

'Wrong again.'

His wing-tendrils told her his anger had ebbed but now it was her tendrils that doused the way ahead with light. 'So what have you *learned*,' she demanded.

'That at the end of this riven, is a circular space that when filled with zlat blossom, makes the glass-stones look like eggs in a giant nest. You come here, I learned, because you want to hatch young.'

The claim was so preposterous Genn actually laughed. 'I come here because the glass-stones are beautiful or at least they were.'

'No more beautiful than glass-stones in a dozen other rivens I could name. The she-dragon obviously thought it was a good nest site too, which is why she came here to hatch her brood, although things turned out less well for her than they will for you. When you nest, Genn, I'll be by your side to protect you.'

The dragon egg flexed as the sprite struggled against its confines and Genn feared it was about to break free.

'No response?' goaded Orin. 'Surely you're going to deny wanting young?'

'Wanting young doesn't mean wanting you,' she muttered distractedly.

'I sense you have some interest in me or I wouldn't have persisted.'

'It's unwise to trust your senses, Orin.'

'They've served me well so far. I sensed you'd come here after you breached axeel and you did, and I sensed you'd be antagonistic, and you are.'

'Even Lyt knows where I go and what I feel.'

Orin's wing-tendrils flashed crimson as he rounded on her. 'Why won't you *accept* me, Genn?' Orin had never asked her outright before and for a moment she was too taken aback to respond. 'Genn?'

'You aren't a nester.'

'You don't know that!'

'Tell me I'm wrong,' she challenged.

'You're wrong.'

'Prove it,' she flung back at him.

'I can't prove it unless you *accept* me,' he cried in frustration.

'True. So I suppose I'll never know.'

'You don't *want* to know,' he said more calmly, as they went on. 'It takes commitment to nest, from a Waiwin *and* a Velven, but you use your *so-called* doubts over my commitment to camouflage your *own*. You enjoy the freedom to come and go as you please more than the young you profess to want. It's *convenient* to blame me for your *own* flaw.'

'Not all Velven or Waiwin choose to nest,' she retorted, stung by his words. 'It isn't a flaw to remain alone.'

'The flaw I refer to is self-delusion not solitariness.' She said nothing and he gentled his voice. 'Both Velven and

Waiwin have the right to live alone but I ceased to enjoy it long ago. I want something more and I think you do as well.'

There was a long silence and it was Orin who broke it. 'Maybe my chase has gone on too long and defeating me has become a game to you, but what's the winner's prize, Genn? An egg that belongs to another mother? A youngster that will never be yours? Or is that the attraction? That the hatchling you carry next to your heart will only ever be temporary?'

Genn stumbled to a stop and he stepped closer breaking axeel. 'What do you really want that you don't trust me to provide?'

'You can have any Velven you desire, Orin, and you've had many,' she said tightly. 'And if we speak of habits, then yours is to take what you want and fly away, as free as the wind. And it isn't a habit you'll break.'

His wing-tendrils surged with a crimson as bright as fire, but it was the faint wash of light ahead that revealed his face and with it, the true depth of his anger. It told her he would never accept her summation of him. 'The cavern ends,' she said.

'But not our time in it,' he grated as he stared in the same direction. 'There are more flintsaurs in front than behind.'

Orin was right! Their crests formed a jagged silhouette against the light as they milled about the cavern's opening. 'So many of them,' she whispered. 'I don't understand.'

'I do,' snapped Orin. 'They smell a dragon-corpse which tells them there's a feast to be had at the tunnel's far end except, thanks to their friends, there isn't, just a Velven and Waiwin as consolation snacks in the middle.'

'They're coming,' hissed Genn, as the silhouettes advanced.

'Toss them the egg and we can slide out overhead while they squabble over it,' he ordered.

30

But the prospect of killing the dragon sprite was even worse now she'd felt its movements. 'They aren't having the sprite!'

'Then you slide out while they squabble over me.'

'You won't survive!'

'I'm the strongest and fastest of the Waiwin,' said Orin grimly.

'There are too many of them!'

His eyes were blacker than night and he caught her by the shoulders, breaching axeel and every other convention she could think of. 'I'm no longer free as the wind,' he ground out. 'I care only that you escape!'

He vaulted into the air and flew straight at them and she saw flintsaurs leap and miss him, then catch his leg. Almost he managed to shrug himself free but more leapt, snagged his wing, and dragged him down.

'Orin!' she screamed and launched into the air. The flintsaurs formed a seething mass as they fought over their prize and with an anguished cry, she hurled the dragon egg at them, and then the world exploded in flame.

For a moment she had no idea what had happened and then she realised the sprite had burst from its shell and now blasted the flintsaurs with fire as if, by some quirk of egg-memory, it knew its mother's fate. All Genn knew was if the flintsaurs hadn't killed Orin, the dragon sprite would and her as well.

The flintsaurs abandoned Orin in a bid to save their scaly skins and Genn landed beside him. He was motionless, soaked in blood, and too heavy to lift. All she could do was stand guard over him while the sprite methodically went about its grisly work. The air filled with the stench of burned flesh and the flintsaurs' smoldering corpses rose in a macabre wall around them until the scrape of flintsaur claws on stone was replaced with the crack of settling bones.

The sprite's fire finally ceased and it circled above, as if to admire its handiwork, and then it ceased its circling and hovered. Genn held her breath as she stared up, powerless to stop it incinerating her and Orin. The sprite's ruby eyes looked deeply into hers and then, with a flick of its tail, it powered away. Some sort of understanding had passed between them, Genn realised dazedly, but she hardly knew what.

'That went better than expected,' croaked Orin, and Genn dropped to her knees beside him.

'Really? The flintsaurs have done you a lot of damage, Orin.'

'Nothing that won't mend,' he said, and managed to sit up. 'And not as much damage as the sprite did to them,' he added, and surveyed the carnage. 'It's built us a nest of roasted flintsaurs.'

Genn grimaced. 'Not the kind of nest I had in mind.'

'Nor I.' There was a long pause. 'You traded the egg for me.'

Orin's eyes were still black and Genn felt her own darken. 'I was only ever its temporary mother.'

He considered her for a long moment. 'Does that mean you *accept* me?'

'It means I've broken my habit.'

'And do you think I've broken mine?'

'Do you?' she asked quietly.

'Yes, but that's for you to judge.'

Genn made no reply, she simply let her wings rise and curve towards him as she had long wanted to. His rose too, more slowly than hers, not just because he was injured but because he was determined to let her choose. Her aqua wing-tendrils reached out to his crimson ones and Genn sighed as they entwined and a sweet surge passed between them.

32

Her tendrils were no longer aqua but amethyst, as Orin's were, a hue that was theirs alone and marked them as true-locked, and they remained so, black eyes staring into black eyes. 'What now Orin?' she asked softly.

He smiled. 'Now we build a nest.'

Dragon Sprite Deep Fantasy Retelling

Writers can be broadly classified as planners or pantsers, and I'm a pantser. As the name suggests, writers in the first group don't start writing their short story, novel, novel series etc without a plan. The plan might be just a rough plot and/or chapter outline, or a few jotted points, or might be very detailed indeed, like the highly prescriptive plans/ structures listed online that dictate the word count when a certain action takes place and/or when a secondary character appears. In contrast, pantsers (as in flying by the seat of their pants) simply start to write to see where the story takes them.

I've only ever planned one of my 17 novels (*I Heard the Wolf Call My Name*) because it followed on from my *Angel Caste* series where I'd struggled to pull together 300,000 plus (unplanned) words into a meaningful ending. I dreaded repeating the exhausting and unnerving experience so I grudgingly wrote out thirty chapter outlines and then, bored witless by now knowing what the story was about (and thus having no reason to write it), abandoned them and pantsered a story where only the main character's name remained the same.

Even so, planning and pantsering aren't mutually exclusive. Planners are no less likely than pantsers to experience that magic moment when a story takes on a life of its own (not the one they planned) and pantsers often reach the point where at least some planning is necessary. In my struggle to conclude the five book *Angel Caste* series, I wrote the ending first and then backfilled the three chapter gap. (There's actually no rules about what order you have to write a story in!)

You would expect Deep Fantasy elements to be more common in the works of pantsers than planners, given pantsers write with less conscious intent but Deep Fantasy elements also emerge in planned stories. For instance, I've read that Ursula Le Guin had no knowledge of Carl Jung's concept of the Shadow when she wrote the ending of *A Wizard of Earthsea* noted previously and, given her set writing regime, I'm guessing she wasn't a pantser.

Dragon Sprite sprang from a want to play with the popular fantasy trope of fairies and I had fairies in mind, with their association with tiny beauty, not the faeries/Fae/elves/Little Folk and their associations with (sometimes malevolent) power. I find human variations (think Tolkien's hobbits, elves, dwarves, trolls, orcs, goblins, Men of Westernesse, Tom Bombadil and Goldberry) interesting on a range of levels including the question of what it means to be human and, despite choosing the fairy trope, I wanted to write something different.

The story led me from Genn's sap-covered claws, via a trail of broken eggshells, into the liminal (the cavern), but Deep Fantasy elements had emerged well before then, though I didn't notice all of them at the time. These included the zlat blossom (suggesting later fruit), the glass-stones (mimicking eggs/future life), and the dragon (symbol of creative earth energies and producer of the eggs/future life). The flintsaurs' consumption of the she-dragon mimics the circle of life (death feeding life) which is echoed by the spherical glass-stones in the circular dish of land that, as Orin points out, resembles a nest (the nurturing space of new life).

It's worth noting that prior to Christianity making the pagan Western dragon into a symbol of evil to be slain by the purer might of the Christian church (in the guise of Saint George), Western dragons were similar to Asian dragons (long/loong/lung) who retain their links to the divine to this day.

Genn is drawn into the cavern (liminal) in the conscious hope of finding an unbroken egg (a reflection of her unconscious yearning for her own young). She protects the egg she finds as she would her own offspring despite its dangers but as Orin correctly claims, the dragon sprite meets her mothering urges while allowing her to remain her old, solitary self.

Orin is also on a journey to a new life stage. Despite his reputation as promiscuous and untrustworthy, he invests time trying to understand Genn, declares he is tired of being alone, and insightfully perceives many of Genn's motivations. He follows her into the cavern (the liminal), in spite of its obvious dangers and it is there that both he and Genn confront their respective Shadows via a heated exchange. In essence, both struggle with the fear of connecting/joining (their future life stages).

The struggles of the hero (in the universal hero myth identified by Joseph Campbell) sometimes culminate in a crisis or final ordeal which dramatically forces the hero to finally enter their new psychological state/life stage and so it is with Genn and Orin. In the desperate moment of the flintsaur attack, Orin sacrifices himself (dies to his old self to be born to his new self) to save Genn, and Genn hurls away the precious dragon egg to save Orin, (sacrifices her autonomy/pseudo motherhood). Thus, in the liminal space of the cavern, they assimilate their Shadows to be rewarded with the life stages they crave.

WEREWOMAN

My friends used to call me werewoman. It was a joke because I disappeared whenever the moon was full and liked to eat my meat rare. They were closer to the truth than they knew but I'm no shape-shifter. My heart's never changed but it's grown harder to hide the fact that I'm not fully human either. When the moon hangs large in the sky I become like its reflection on moving water; continuously broken and put back together again.

The moon liberates and taunts me with my captivity. It pulls at my blood like an owl pulls at the entrails of small, furred things. As a child, I didn't understand it was the moon's swell that triggered dreams that made me run and hunt and give voice, smash my foster sisters' dolls and kill their pets and, when all else failed, mutilate myself.

After each *unfortunate incident*, I was moved on to another foster home until I was placed in government *care* and, by the time I was sixteen, I was on the streets. I ran with a pack at first, finding a kind of safety in the company of others, and I fooled myself I'd found a new world, my world, but people only play at wildness, while always seeking shelter. Except Davin perhaps. His blood seemed riddled with the same wild yearnings as mine and when his furred chest pressed down on mine and my legs locked him close, I thought I'd found my world but I was left hungry, always hungry, and the dreams kept coming.

I left Davin long ago. I'm older now and my understanding of the moon's demands clearer. My dreams are clearer too. What I seek isn't to be found in the paved ways of cities, or even in the ever moving oceans, but in the mountains' deeper darkness.

I start my walk along the highway when the moon grows full. I've walked this way countless times before but tonight will be my last. I wear the summer dress that clings to my breasts and flicks up to reveal my thighs and it's never long before a car or truck stops to carry me closer to where I must go.

Their male drivers think of what lies between my legs. I see it in the way they moisten their lips and smell it in their sweat but I'm not afraid. My jaws can crush the windpipe of any male whose wariness is swamped by desire.

The male who picks me up tonight is middle-aged. His scalp shines through his pelt and his sinewy hand brushes my knee as he changes gears. His wedding ring catches the moonlight too as he gestures at the way ahead and tells me how far he travels each day, each month, each year. I only care about my own journeys and keep my lips firmly closed and my manicured hands folded in my lap.

'You can drop me here,' I say, when the time is right. He looks surprised but pulls over. It's a long way from the city and longer still to the next town. He seems about to protest or offer me fatherly advice but my eyes catch the moonlight and he thinks better of it.

I remain where I am until his tail-lights disappear into the darkness. I hear other vehicles too, off in the distance and small animals on the run through the undergrowth. I smell their blood as it pulses through their fragile veins and, as I move deeper into the trees, I'm barely aware of discarding my clothes or where they land. In the past I kept careful note of such things but not tonight. This time there'll be no returning.

I loose my hair and it slides down my naked back as sensuous as a mounting he-wolf then set off in a lope. Fronds whip my flanks and my eyes become the hunters' eyes of snakes and owls, and of the hunted, things with soft underbellies and succulent flesh. The air is full of scent-stories of blood and dung and death.

The ground steepens but I don't slow, driven by needs unshaped by thought. Time passes but time is a human thing. All I know is each thrust of bone and sinew brings me closer to my destination.

The slope ends in a cave and my neck pelt shifts. I've been to this part of the forest many times but never seen a cave. The opening is darker than night, as if it draws in light but doesn't release it. I flare my nostrils but there's no scent to guide me as I'm pulled forward by the same force that pulled me here.

The air's heavy and still and while I know my feet rise and fall, I feel no sense of movement. I want to stop but stopping's not possible. Then there's a pool, the moon's reflection adrift on its surface, despite the sealed roof.

'You've been a long time coming.'

The voice echoes in my head and I start. 'Show yourself!' I growl.

Look into the pool,' the voice instructs.

I'm compelled forward and the gleam of my eyes disturbs the moon's paler reflection, then both shimmer away and there's another face, human but not human, its eyes slit with a cat's pupil. I recoil but the compulsion to stay is like a boot on my throat.

'Dream,' the voice insists.

I'm back in the cool night air, sometimes in the mind of the cat-eyed creature, sometimes hovering like a hawk above it. Its thoughts mimic mine in my journey up the mountain but are more scattered, as if less tied to human patterns.

I thrill to its beauty as it bounds up the slope and stops at a cave. It's the same cave I'm in, I realise with a jolt. The creature disappears inside and I'm in its head again, seeing with its eyes. A similar creature to it awaits but hulking and sinister. I recoil and for a moment, am lost in the darkness.

'Dream!' The order binds me and I'm back in the cat-eyed creature's head.

'It comes,' the hulking creature says, and I snarl in anger and fear.

There's a blink of blackness then I'm in the forest, a hawk again, watching a woman. She's in a clearing next to a pool, her long hair and naked skin wet as if she's lately swum. I know it's my mother though I have no memory of her and as the cat-creature steps from the trees, I know I'm about to witness my own conception.

Fear surges and I'm back in the cave. I've seen terrifying pictures of men hunting wolves and as a child, dreamed of wolf-wraiths: skinless, blood-clad, doomed to roam forever under shelterless skies.

'There's always been others,' the hulking creature confirms. 'The changling, the wild-child, the shifter, the werewolf, and in the end, they come here, as you have, in search of a new world.'

'And do they find it?' My hoarse voice is scarcely more than a growl.

'They go the way of the pool and do not return.'

The moon's face shimmers on water black and cold and fathomless, but I think of the moon of stone in the other world outside, where men hunt, and kill, and thieve the hides of wolves and I leap and power ever deeper into the water. Flesh collapses inwards and bone compresses until I'm an arrowhead of stone arcing towards death. I pass into nothingness and then the colour of the water slowly changes. Agate emerges first, then emerald, then bright green and with a final thrust, I'm back in a sunlit day. I float on my back, a husk as ephemeral as the butterflies that dance above, drift to shore and step from the water. A creature emerges into the open and heat flares in my groin. A new world is about to begin.

40

Werewoman Deep Fantasy Retelling

Over time I've come to believe that we live a series of lives not a single changing one. Our earliest memories, kindergarten perhaps, primary school, secondary school, university, different relationships, different houses, different jobs all so distinct that each produces different versions of ourselves.

In one of my previous lives, I was the Foundation Head of a writing and publishing degree, and in that role, was surprised by my undergraduates' frequent disdain for Stephenie Meyer's *The Twilight Saga*. When pressed, they'd cite the poor writing or plot or premise, or all three. They weren't judgements I shared (nor were shared by millions of readers and viewers) but given the series' phenomenal success, I suspected something else was at play in the works apart from an engaging story.

The titles of the main books: *Twilight*, *New Moon*, *Eclipse* and *Breaking Dawn*, immediately suggested the liminal but it was Bella's love interests that really drew my attention: Jacob the werewolf (symbolising our animal nature), and Edward the vampire (symbolising the undying divinity of our higher consciousness/spirit/soul) (though he doesn't reach God-like/gods-like status because his need of blood keeps him tethered to his human/animal aspect).

There has long been a perceived division between our animal and divine elements, at least in Western culture, a tension reflected in the term human animal. As primates, we share 99% of our DNA with our closest cousins (chimpanzees and bonobos) a relationship that sits uncomfortably with religious doctrines claiming humans are made in God's image (and superior to the lesser creatures of the animal kingdom). Yet human bodies are undeniably animal and, unlike the immortality

41

of God/gods, are subject to disease, decay and death.

I wondered whether Bella's difficulty (in *The Twilight Saga*) in choosing between the animal of Jacob and the higher consciousness/spirit/soul of Edward, provides readers with a tool (at the unconscious level) to reconcile the same opposing elements within themselves.

Many religions resolve this dilemma by splitting humans in two (which might be what Stephenie Meyer does in the characters of Jacob/Edward). Our animal body corrupts and dies, while our consciousness/spirit/soul, being divine, lives on. This duality of the body and soul is apparent in entities such as angels that combine the animal (human shape) and the divine (wings that literally and metaphorically allow angels to rise above/transcend their human form).

The human-animal divide isn't the only duality Western cultures have difficulties with, another being the nature of male and femaleness. Jung suggests the human psyche contains both female (anima) and male (animus) aspects, which seems logical given the composite nature of the human physical body. There are myths that resolve this male/female tension by splitting the human entity in two, thus giving us the male-female twins of Osiris and Isis in Egyptian mythology, Apollo and Artemis in Greek mythology, and Freyr and Freyja in Scandinavian mythology, while StarWars provides a more contemporary example in Luke and Leia.

I employ a variation of the twin archetype in my The *Kira Chronicles* series to reconcile the male-female, killing-healing aspects of humans. The series tells of twin gold-eyed princes, one warrior, one healer, whose descendants (the gold-eyed warrior Tierken and the gold-eyed healer Kira) must join to reconcile their male/female - killer/healer aspects to save their respective peoples by reuniting/rebalancing them.

These same themes are played out in *Werewoman*. The protagonist leaves the highway (the conscious world) and enters the forest/cave/pool, the liminal spaces where her movement to the next life stage takes place. Even before that, the moon triggers dreams that hint of what is to come and its reflection in the pool (despite the cave's ceiling) confirms she's in the unconscious. The importance of the moon, with its links to the feminine, introduces the Ancient Greek philosophical notion of Eros and Logos, the former broadly creativity/chaos and the latter rationality/order. Unsurprisingly, Jung saw Eros as feminine and Logos as masculine.

During the werewoman's time in the liminal space (unconscious), she confronts the creatures in her Shadow which are simultaneously parts of herself and separate (she sees through the creature's eyes and observes it from above). In a similar vein, in Le Guin's *A Wizard of Earthsea*, Ged's Shadow (Ged) is separate but also part of him. And like Gandalf in his battle with his Shadow/Balrog (in *The Lord of the Rings*), the werewoman must 'die to her old self' to become her new self.

While the moon links to her anima (female aspect of her psyche) both the 'cat-cyed creature' and the 'hulking creature' in the cave, are parts of her animus (the male aspect of her psyche). Both order or encourage her (along with moon) to dream, in order to advance her journey of transformation because dreams draw on the same helpful metaphors, symbols and archetypes as myths found in the unconscious. Or as Joseph Campbell famously said: dream is the personalised myth, myth the depersonalised dream. The werewoman 'dies to her old self' and returns to the world 'a husk', empty of what she was before. As she floats on the surface of the pool (consciousness/ real world), butterflies (symbols of transformation given their metamorphosis from caterpillar to butterfly) 'dance above' to reinforce the idea of change. The final scene replicates her own conception, the result of the joining of a 'lower' animal (the body) with a 'higher' human (divine consciousness) but having reconciled her animal-human elements, the werewoman is at peace with her new life stage.

Finally, the term *were*woman (an allusion to the better known *were*wolf) actually means manwoman (*were* being the archaic word for an adult male) and so the werewoman's new state suggests she's not only reconciled her animal/higher consciousness aspects, but her male and female aspects (animus/anima) as well.

FALLEN

Fallen I

At first she thought it was a swan, its feathers shining in the sun as it struggled in the sky, but then she remembered that the swans here were black and this bird was white. She squinted up at it while Mitzy barked furiously behind her, straining on her chain. The chickens clucked and fussed, and she half turned, worried she'd forgotten to feed them again but then there was a crash and she jumped. Whatever it was had come down beyond the knoll and, heart in mouth, she hobbled into the trees.

The crutch pap had made for her found holes under the leaves and she fell and whimpered at the thought of snakes that might hide there, big ones with black skins and red bellies, and ones as stripy as tigers. On a hot day like today, they'd be out and about in search of food.

She managed to haul herself up and drag her gaze back to the trees ahead. There was something white there, a goose maybe like mam said they had back Home, but it was too big even for a goose and she drew a sharp breath. It was man, lying face down, and he was naked! Her faltering gaze took in his wings, splayed out, one clearly broken and she dropped to her knees, hands clamped over her eyes.

'Holy Mary, Mother of God!' she muttered over and over again. Mam had told her about angels often enough, especially Gabriel, who came for wicked children, but despite her terror, she was reminded of the baby sparrow she'd found.

'Mama birds throw the poorly from the nest,' mam had told her, so maybe the angel had come to take her, for she was poorly too. She cowered lower. *No!* she screamed silently. *No! No! No!*

Nothing happened and when she finally summonsed the courage to peek through her fingers, the angel had gone.

Fallen II

She guessed it was a parachute, for she'd seen them on the newsreels at the pictures but the war wasn't here, it was in Darwin, far away. Maybe the man's plane had been driven off course and he'd run out of fuel. Maybe he was The Enemy. Whoever he was, he was in trouble, coming down fast, his chute empty of air. He disappeared beyond the rise and she heard a crash, then she limped into the trees, heart racing.

The brace chafed at her as it always did and Mitzy barked furiously to be let off the chain. The hens squawked, impatient to be fed, and she felt guilty as she struggled on past. The brace gave rigidity to her withered leg but on hot days like today, it gave her skin a brown stain too.

'Best leave school and work the farm,' dad had said. 'Learning's no use to a woman who's to be a wife.' But no man wanted a cripple for a wife.

The brace had lost its rubber foot and she slipped, almost fell, and then saw white but it was no parachute. It was a dummy like the ones in the shops in town, *except for its wings*, one of which was broken. It had explicit sexual organs too and her face burned.

She guessed it had been thrown from a plane as a joke, for she'd heard on the wireless of the drunken servicemen in Sydney and of their lewdness, but then the dummy sat up, stretched out its whole, unbroken wing, and looked at her with silver eyes. Mitzy's frantic barking increased back at the house and she buried her face in her arms and took refuge in the little knowledge she had.

'Education defeats ignorance,' Mr. Peterson, her old science teacher, had boomed. 'The church once killed people who dared to speak the truth yet insisted on absurdities like angels. Why,' he'd scoffed, his finger jabbing the air, 'to get the weight of a man's body off the ground, an angel's wings would have to be as big as this room.' Her friend Maria had believed in angels but Maria was Catholic and dad said the Mick's believed in all sorts of weird things, like not eating meat on Fridays.

'There are no such things as angels,' she chanted silently, and when she was at last able to raise her head, the sunny space was empty.

Fallen III

At first she thought it was a weather balloon, its foil glinting in the sun as it dropped, and then a hang-glider, one wing broken, the rider struggling to save it and himself. It disappeared into the gums with a crash that sent the cockatoos and galahs screeching into the air. She lumbered into the scrub and stopped in astonishment. There was no sign of a hang-glider, just an angelic version of Michelangelo's statue of David.

His skin was like polished marble, his hair scrolled around his face, his large eyes closed, his mouth small, his chest, torso, narrow hips and genitals as perfect as David's. She might have even believed he was a statue, some piece of mishandled airline cargo, had it not been for his wings. They were like a swan's, immense and snowy, but one was fractured, its jagged pinions soaked with blood.

The vivid red against the white reminded her of when a fox had carried off Hettie and left behind a bloodied wing. At the time she'd been grateful the chook was dead and wouldn't have to drag itself on through life lop-sided like she did.

The angel remained still and she pondered whether angels breathed or had sex. It was hard to imagine that perfect phallus erect, pulsing with blood, and no longer pure. God might have made angels in human form, apart from their wings, but surely their genitals were more decorative than functional?

She reached her good hand towards his shoulder and stopped, not wanting to contaminate him. They didn't have bacteria in Heaven, did they? Or coughs, or colds, or strokes? His eyes opened and she lurched backwards and landed with a thump on her backside. His irises were silver and she wondered whether he saw as she did or whether his vision was God-given, and he already judged her and found her wanting.

'Are you hurt?' she managed to ask, needing to break the silence, but given his wing, the question was ridiculous. 'Are you in pain?' she amended, annoyed she slurred. Her speech was always worse when she was tired and clambering through the bush had exhausted her.

The angel stood in a single, graceful motion, his muscles making his skin ripple like milk, and she struggled upright too. He was twice as tall as her and she was seized with a fear he'd been sent to take her. But she couldn't go now! Not with the chooks still to be fed and Mitzy still on her chain!

The angel started to shrink until he was just a little taller than her and she was able to think again. If he could rearrange his body like that, surely he could mend his broken wing? But it still draggled in the gum leaves, bloodied and useless. Then he shrugged, like a bird before it settles for the night, and smiled. 'I misread the direction of the wind,' he said.

His mouth hadn't moved but the words hung in her head like silvery chimes. 'Didn't you have divine guidance?' she said. No reply appeared in her head and she tried again. 'Would you like to come back to the house?' Her speech was almost as formless as Mitzy's yapping but the angel seemed to understand.

He nodded and fell into step beside her, slowing when she staggered sideways, and stopping when she fell and had to use the scrub to heave herself up. He didn't help or send silvery words of sympathy and she bad-temperedly wondered whether his heart was marble too.

Mitzy's barking doubled as they emerged from the gums and she ruffled the dog's ears with her good hand. 'I won't let her off the chain,' she mumbled. 'Mitzy doesn't like strangers.'

'She won't mind me,' sent the angel and he was right. Once free, Mitzy set off on her usual round through the bush as though he didn't exist.

She struggled to the chook-shed and tossed a half pan of wheat through the wire. The chooks emerged from the shade into the sun-bleached dust and she crooned to them before she led the angel into the house.

It was little more than a shack, with no fridge or television, and no electricity since a storm had taken out the back *and* the power pole but there was always enough food for her and Mitzy and the chooks. The angel stopped on the threshold. 'Come in,' she slurred. 'It's not very grand. It was better before the storm.'

'I know. I saw it,' sent the angel, and followed her in.

'You've been here before?' She knew her speech was unintelligible and that the angel understood it anyhow.

'Yes. But this is the first time I've been invited in.'

She shivered as she wondered whether she'd invited in Death. The angel's beauty shone like a lamp but she supposed the Angel of Death didn't go about looking like the Grim Reaper of popular fiction. 'Why did you come here before?' she whispered, fearing the worse.

'To get my wing fixed.'

She stared at him in astonishment. 'But … didn't you injure it just now when you hit the gum trees?'

'It's been broken a long time.'

'Can't God mend it?'

'God prefers we mend things ourselves.'

That sounded about right, she thought sourly. After the stroke, her well-meaning friends had prayed on her behalf, or insisted she pray for healing because, after all, she had by some miracle been spared death. Even the doctors said a brain-bleed as catastrophic as hers inevitably killed people and to prove the point, procured a priest to administer the last rites. Being mute and paralysed meant she'd had to lay there and endure them but she *had* prayed later, when she'd escaped back here and the stroke had stopped her properly caring for Mitzy and the chooks.

Dear Lord, make me as I was before but the lifeless side of her body remained lifeless. Even in dreams she was an ill-balanced, shambling mess. So much for God! She flushed as she recalled the angel heard her thoughts and that he was God's emissary.

'Why didn't you mend your wing on an earlier visit?' she asked, hoping to distract him from her rudeness.

'The time wasn't right. There was too much fear and ignorance.'

He sounded like those self-help books her friends had foisted on her. How reaching for the strength within and having faith in yourself fixed things. 'What makes you think I can mend it?' she demanded, almost angry. 'I've been useless since the stroke. It would've been better had God taken all of me instead of only half.'

'You're good with chooks. The task's the same only bigger.'

She actually laughed then, the unfamiliar sound shockingly loud to her ears. 'If I bind your wing, you'll have to stay and wait for it to heal and I don't know how long it'll take. Some things don't heal for a very long time, or they never heal, no matter how hard you try.'

'That's true,' sent the angel.

She sighed as she considered how hard it was just to rise each day and that if it weren't for Mitzy and the chooks she wouldn't bother. 'I'll try,' she said reluctantly, but all she wanted was to take to her bed. The angel waited patiently while she tore up a sheet and laboriously bound the broken pinions and she was trembling with fatigue by the time she'd finished but oddly triumphant.

'You should sleep,' sent the angel.

She nodded and collapsed onto the old couch too exhausted to even reach the bed. The angel watched her motionless. It was quiet outside, as if the chooks and Mitzy slept too. The setting sun found the window and filled the room with reds and golds, and then ebbed to be replaced with the cooler white of stars but still the angel didn't move. He simply stood, as pale and cold as stone.

At precisely midnight, he unfolded his wings, stretched them to their fullest width, and beat them. The bindings fell to the floor like heavy snow but she didn't wake and he stilled his wings and went to the couch. In sleep, she looked as beautiful as him, her pain and frustration smoothed away, her symmetry restored by the room's shadows.

He raised his wings and brought them down over her like an immense, sheltering hand. 'Thank you,' he sent, and in her dream, she ran as light and free as sunshine through the gums.

Fallen Deep Fantasy Retelling

I explored the nature of angels at length in my *Angel Caste* fantasy series where the protagonist, Viv, a half human-half angel, fights to find a place for herself in the world. While Viv's struggle is very much that of reconciling her human and angelic elements (a common symbolic meaning of angels discussed earlier), the main angelic character (Thris) also has a quest. He must rise through the angelic hierarchy and then transcend, a goal achieved by performing good deeds. But as time goes on, he comes to understand that what makes a deed *good* is far from clear and that he, as well as the angels supposed to help him, might be prone to the very human flaws of lust, jealousy, and self-serving ambition.

In *Fallen*, a damaged angel appears to a damaged woman living in isolated poverty in the Australian bush but the *effects* of the angel's appearance vary depending on the time of his appearance. In his first visit, fear closes the door to what he offers, and on his second visit, science does. On his third visit, the woman is able to overcome her fears and be open to the mysteries he presents. She is at last psychologically ready to *invite* him in, that is, be open to psychological healing.

The angel is a symbol of the woman's wounded psyche, however, her physical wounds are more obvious and mirrored in the broken down house (a common metaphor for the physical body). The fact that there is always food and warmth in the house and her love and care for the dog and chooks, shows she hasn't given up physically and that her damaged psyche is capable of being healed.

Her psychological wounds are more limiting than her physical ones. She's angry with God, the medical profession, and her friends, but has reached the point of wanting to heal (move onto her next life stage). Despite her fears the angel represents Death (which he does, the death of her previous angry and unhappy life stage), she invites him in.

The physical act of binding the angel's wing is part of a process of psychological healing (accepting her physical state) which is why she feels triumphant afterwards and her (almost unnaturally) deep sleep allows her psychological healing to be completed. At precisely midnight (a liminal space, discussed earlier) the angel brings his (whole/ undamaged) wings over her in a gesture of safety and so completes her journey of psychological healing, reflected in her dream of physical wholeness and freedom.

A PRINCE LOST IN A JUNGIAN DREAM

The Prince descended step by step until he reached a cave then stopped and gulped wetly, overcome by memories of entrapment.

'Enter,' a voice boomed and the Prince crept forward. The dim shape of the Wise Old Man emerged from the gloom, his stern face lit by flames from a fire circle. 'I have been waiting for you,' he said, and gestured to a couch. 'You may sit, or lie down if it comforts you.'

'I will sit,' croaked the Prince, and perched on the edge of the plush upholstery.

The Wise Old Man steepled his slender fingers and the Prince's broad-tipped ones tightened on his knees. 'Start at the beginning,' ordered the Wise Old Man.

'The golden ball crashed down into my world,' began the Prince.

'That is not the beginning.'

The Prince scowled. 'I never liked the egg,' he said.

'Why?'

'It limited me. I was glad to be rid of it. The tail was no better. I was glad to lose it too and gain my legs.'

'Why?'

Were the reasons not obvious, thought the Prince sourly. 'The tail confined me to water but the legs allowed me to travel the lands.'

'So, once you had shed your former selves, you were content?'

'It was an improvement.' He paused. 'And then the golden ball crashed down into my world.' He smiled an oily, shovel-cut smile. 'Its owner was very sorry to lose it.'

'You offered to retrieve it?' The Prince nodded. 'For a price?'

'It had gone down to where unwanted things settle in rank layers. It was reasonable to be compensated.'

The Wise Old Man's brows lowered but the Prince was lost in pleasurable memories. 'The Princess was fair but did not think *me* so and yet she promised me much in return for her precious ball. There was to be food from her plate and a place in her bed.' The Prince smirked. 'The morsels she ate, I ate too, and the silk sheets she slept between, I slept between too. I cleaved to her that night and was changed and so she thought me fairer and, as time passed, she cleaved to *me*, closer and closer.'

'And were you content?'

'Her love grew as suffocating as the egg.'

'Love makes us whole,' said the Wise Old Man.

The Prince shrugged. 'I escaped to a forest so perilous even the King's men dare not follow.'

'She released you.'

'I *escaped*!'

'You were an ugly thing that came from the deep. She made you her companion and so, over time, you became beautiful to her. She came to love you as she loved herself and, being whole, was able to let you go.'

The Prince's mouth stretched wire-thin. 'I *escaped* to a forest untouched by axe, a shadow-land where demons dwelt, things ill-birthed and part-formed, cast from the light. They were thick about me but I forced my way through.'

'They recognised you and let you pass.'

'I *escaped* the egg, the shape that kept me water-bound, the Princess's sweet captivity, and the demons of the wildwoods!'

'And yet you are *here*,' observed the Wise Old Man.

The Prince's throat thrummed in agitation as he stared at the enclosing walls. 'I … I found something deep in that forest.' The fire danced in the stone circle, but it was another circle that had drawn him, one rimmed with mines that rang with the chime of picks. And there, at its centre, was a coffin, worked as a jewel might be: faceted, bright with light, sparkling.

He had approached it half in horror, half in hope and within it had lain the most exquisite maid. He had thought her dead at first, despite her perfection, but she slept. The coffin was seamless as if the maid had lived her entire life confined but he had escaped many a prison and sensed the maid's wish to escape her own.

His soft hands had imprinted its crystal surface with a power that sprang from the water's green depths and the forest's deep roots and, as the lid lifted away, her eyes opened, gold-green like his. He had told her his story to win her trust, and she had told him hers.

She had been a child in a mighty castle and then a maid with a new mother who was cruel and uncaring and later, intent on harm. There had been just one mirror in the castle and the new mother had made it her own. The forest had promised another mirror, where the maid could finally know herself, but the path had taken her ever deeper into the darkness. 'She was so beautiful,' finished the Prince thickly.

'And yet you are *here*,' repeated the Wise Old Man.

'She would not leave.'

'And you would not stay.'

'The darkness held nothing for me!'

'She was there,' the Wise Old Man reminded him.

'With her servants, blunt-faced and stubby, besmirched with what they hacked and hewed. Not fitting for her.' His throat thrummed like the flick of a moth's wing half-devoured. 'She told me they cared for her, dug for her.' His thin lips twisted. 'She remains like a flower, frozen in ice, neither living nor dying, and so they dig ever deeper to free her.' The Prince's gold-green eyes flashed. 'I need her here with me!'

'And she needs you there with her.'

The Prince's muscles bunched as if he would leap from the couch. 'I tried to return to her but could not find the way,' he said hoarsely. 'That is why I am here.'

'But where is here?' The Prince blinked in confusion. 'You must go deeper,' said the Wise Old Man and gestured to steps, barely visible in the floor.

The Prince looked at them fearfully. 'And will I find her again?'

'If you dig like those others.'

'There were seven.'

'And soon will be eight.'

'You will be here?' asked the Prince uncertainly.

The Wise Old Man nodded. 'I am your Guide. I will always be with you.'

A Prince Lost in a Jungian Dream Deep Fantasy Retelling

While some fairy stories, folk tales, and nursery rhymes have survived for hundreds of years, most have changed over time as expected. While written versions of *Cinderella* can be traced back to fifth century China and contemporary versions continue to be produced in the form of popular films like *Pretty Woman* (1990) and *Notting Hill* (1999), the latter with a male Cinderella, the hacking off of flesh from feet and the pecking out of eyes in *Aschenputtel*, an earlier version of *Cinderella*, are long gone.

The Grimm brothers (mid 1700's to mid 1800's) are probably the best known historical collectors and publishers of folk/fairy tales and Disney has continued the tradition in the modern era but both adjusted various tales for commercial reasons and/or to accommodate their target market's sensitivities.

Yet core elements of many stories remain identifiable, even if their representations have changed. In *Aschenputtel*, *Cinderella* seeks solace in a tree which grows from her mother's grave, while in later versions, she seeks solace from a Fairy Godmother (an odd contradiction in terms which hints at a more pagan tradition), but both the tree and the fairy godmother reflect an older, feminine wisdom (the female equivalent of the Wise Old Man archetype). A range of other elements have also survived which *A Prince Lost in a Jungian Dream* explores.

The Frog Prince visits his psychiatrist to sort out his problems but in a Deep Fantasy sense, he descends into his unconscious (symbolised by the cave) to seek aid from the Wise Old Man archetype in his Shadow, located there because the Wise Old Man forces the Prince to confront uncomfortable things about himself. While my story is about the transition of the Frog Prince to a new life stage, the fairy tale of *The Frog Prince* focuses on the Princess's life-stage transition.

In a common version of the story, the Princess is sitting by a well, playing with her golden ball, when she accidentally drops it in the water. Her lamenting brings up a frog, who offers to retrieve the ball if she allows him to eat from her plate and sleep in her bed. Eager for the ball, she agrees, and the frog returns the ball to her. She happily goes off with it, reneging on her bargain, and the frog follows. The King, hearing the frog's complaint, forces his daughter to keep her word and so the frog eats from her plate and then sleeps in her bed where he is transformed into a Prince. In more sanitised versions, the Princess is so disgusted by the frog in her bed she dashes it against the wall and then the transformation takes place.

A Deep Fantasy reading of *The Frog Prince* suggests the Princess is psychologically ready to transition from a daughter to a wife. The frog comes up from her unconscious (the watery depths of the well) bringing to consciousness the precious male animus (golden ball) necessary to her next life stage but she resists (known as Refusal of the Quest in Campbell's hero myth). It is her father who forces her to move from her status as a daughter to her status as a wife (a sexually mature woman).

In contrast, my story focuses on the Prince's inability/refusal to accept and integrate the female aspect of self (the anima) to become whole, and so move to his next life stage. The Wise Old Man (in the guise of the psychiatrist) forces the Prince to retell his life. Firstly the Prince wants to escape the egg (a feminine symbol), and then his tadpole stage so he can walk the land (not dwell in the water – a symbol of the unconscious). The Prince's life journey is outward (conscious) and he neglects/rejects the unconscious, including the Princess, a symbol of the anima again. The Wise Old Man tells the Prince that love makes us whole but, lost in the conscious world, the Prince rejects his words.

His wife, the Princess, having achieved wholeness, lets her reluctant partner go, but the Prince, driven by his dominant male aspect sees his freedom as heroic escape. However, no one can escape the demands of their unconscious forever and when he goes deeper the wild lands of the forest, he journeys ever deeper into his unconscious and his Shadow, where the more primitive parts of self (demons and ill-birthed, part-formed things) dwell.

The Prince prides himself in having escaped the forest (and his wife/anima) but as the Wise Old Man points out, the Prince is still in his unconscious (in the cavern) and so lost he is at last forced to seek help. The Prince recognises consciously the precious thing he must have (his anima in the form of the sleeping girl in the glass coffin) but still denies his unconscious and so doesn't know how to get it.

It's worth noting at this point, how common this archetype of the 'unavailable' anima is in fairy stories. Rapunzel isolated in her tower of stone deep in the forest; Sleeping Beauty ensconced in her castle covered in deadly thorns; Snow White sealed in her coffin of glass. In microcosm, these stories are the knight killing the dragon to rescue the Princess, in other words, the knight overcoming the demons in his Shadow, to claim his anima, and become whole.

The Frog Prince must find his anima (in his unconscious), accept and integrate it, but the twist in this tale is that Snow White is at a similar stage in her journey, a sameness hinted at by their shared eye colour. She has journeyed into a forest's darkness in search of a mirror to finally know herself and the dwarves (creatures of her unconscious), dig for her (continue to seek what she needs deeper in her unconscious) while she remains stuck, in the Prince's words, like a flower, frozen in ice, neither living nor dying.

Snow White is in the liminal (the place between her former life stage and her new one) while the dwarves/her unconscious labour to deliver her to the next life stage. Her present place is one she won't turn back from but one where the Prince refuses to stay. He only realises his mistake later and in desperation, turns to his unconscious for help (the Wise Old Man archetype) who directs him to descend deeper (into his unconscious) via the stairs in the floor and then to dig (as the dwarves do) to go even deeper.

And to help him in this task, as so many are helped in their heroic or mundane quests, is his guide, the Wise Old Man archetype we recognise in Gandalf (from Tolkien's *The Lord of the Rings*), Obi-Wan Kenobi (from Lucas's *Star Wars*), Dumbledor (from Rowling's *Harry Potter* series) and countless other quests where (male) heroes seek transition to their next life stage.

RITE

I've had a bloody long time to get utterly fed up with the rubbish I'm tangled up in, but don't ask me how long, mate, because the dead can't tell the time, can they? And don't ask me who I was before I drowned either, when I was full of life instead of being stuck here, because I don't remember that either. Sometimes I reckon there's more than one of me, as crazy as it sounds, and that I've got mixed up with a whole lot of other blokes who, like me, had their badly thought out plans and half-formed dreams suddenly ripped away.

If you'd asked me then what I wanted to do with my life, I'd have shrugged. That was for the blokes keen to climb the corporate ladder, be the local footy hero, or who'd already traded their freedoms for a wife and kids and a big fat mortgage in some nice little suburb, but I never got the chance for that life either, even *if* I'd wanted it.

My memories have gotten pretty jumbled up over the years. Sometimes I reckon I was a stockman who drowned chasing cattle in a flooded river because some mob of dumb-arsed beasts wasn't going to outsmart me, or I could've been a tradie determined not to let a bit of water over the road stop me getting home on time. I might've even dived into a river I thought was deep, or more likely, not thought beyond beating my mates in, or maybe I did none of these things. Yet in some crazy way I can't explain, I know I died in water and if there's more than one of me, we all went into the water and never bloody well came out.

I mightn't know how I ended up in this place, dead but somehow not dead, and a hell of a long way from anywhere I've been before, but I *do* know where *here* is because it's written on a bloody big sign. The metal's a bit rusty but the writing's clear enough if you bother to read it.

The thing that's caught me like a rat in a trap, is a Quartz Blow, but I call it the *She*. The sign says a whole lot of guff about the chemical reactions that happen when volcanoes decide to fizz and how the chemicals can cause a Quartz Blow but says nothing about how the She keeps me close and knowing *that* would be *really* handy.

If the She *were* just a shinier version of the other piles of rocks around here, I'd be at peace like the dead are supposed to be but instead I'm stuck here between life and death, leashed like the bloody dogs the tourists bring, to stop them wandering off.

The tourists arrive here in their big four-wheel drives complaining about the road, and the dust, and the heat, but go quiet when they see the Blow. The quartz dazzles them but their gawking doesn't last long then they're out and about, climbing up the She's sides, gripping the She's flanks with their sweaty hands, gouging toeholds in the She's skin until they stand on top of her head and imagine they've defeated the thing that's defeated me.

They take pics on their phone cameras to record their triumphs and then drive off taking pieces of the She with them. They choose the sparkly bits, shards that catch the light, but there's a hell of a lot more of the She buried in the darkness under the dirt. It's why I stay up here near the She's shining crown.

The tourists don't care about the parts they can't see and I'm betting they wouldn't care about me either, even if they knew I was here, but I don't blame them. The She's a great lump of glittering quartz whereas I can't even throw a shadow and yet it's the shadows I fear.

The She's dazzling light might drive me crazy but it's a million times better than the water's suffocating darkness that me and the others ended up in. The quartz captures the moonlight and starlight and gives off a milky sheen and as long as I stay nice and close, the world never really gets dark.

Sometimes I think the She only looks sparkly because everything else around here is so bloody dull. Grey-green bushes crowd hard up against grey-green trees and everything's coated with dust stirred up by the four-wheel drives. The bush bakes during the day and is hardly any cooler at night but sometimes dew settles in the early morning, cool and moist, but only in the shadows and I'm too smart to go near them, and so the She keeps her claws in me with hardly any effort at all.

Nothing else around here seems bothered by the darkness. Loud-mouthed crows guard nests all through the night only to hatch fledglings with bottomless bellies who desert in a couple of wingbeats. Dingoes risk the dark too, skulking near highways for roadkill to feed pups who leave to spawn other thankless young in turn. 'Roos slash each other deep in the gullies' gloom to win mates who steal their joeys in a single bound. It's a fool's game but I can't point the finger. It was being a fool that got me marooned here between life and death in the first place.

My frustration builds like summer storms and, like the other blokes who never escaped the water, I feel storms long before they arrive. The air's as tight as fencing wire which means a big one's coming now, but don't get me wrong. I like the rain. It washes everything clean and even when it's tossing it down, it's never truly dark, the light broken into slivers not doused like a billycan of water on a campfire.

I know lightning's coming too and it arrives with nightfall in jagged streaks and booms of thunder that make it hard to think. The rain's even worse, a gigantic roar that turns the blackness deeper than a moonless, starless night. It's like the water's closing over my head all over again and as the darkness swallows the She, snuffing out her light, I make a break for the trees.

It's bloody dark here too but there are odd glimmers of light: the flash of a crow's eyes as its wings shelter its fledglings; the gleam of a dingo's teeth as it scruff-carries its pups from a flooded den; the shine of the roos' wet fur as they crouch over their joeys to shield them from the wet.

Lightning stripes the sky and I suddenly realise a single strike could blast the She to pieces! Rain blinds me but for the first time I see clearly. I'm no crow, or dingo, or 'roo, or anything else that lives but I speed back and stretch my arms out over the She's head. I sense that others do the same despite, like me, fearing a second drowning.

Then something strange happens, too strange to explain, but somehow I know we're all the crow's spread wings, the dingo's safe jaws, and the roos' sheltering backs, and are connected at last, made whole, and set free. The rain still pounds but the thunder and lightning draw away, taking with them their deafening bangs and blinding light. It's dark and wet but for the first time I feel at peace.

The morning brings a clear sky and bushland bright and green. The She's faceted body sparkles and the water trapped in her crevices gleams. The She's beautiful in the light but the She's beautiful in the water-filled darkness too and I linger. For the moment at least, being near her is enough.

Rite Deep Fantasy Retelling

Exploring a quartz blow wasn't on my list when we visited Cobbold Gorge in Outback Far North Queensland (Australia) in October 2021. In fact, despite being an ex-Geographer, I'd never heard of a thing called a quartz blow before the trip. The name intrigued me and so, on a day that edged towards 40C (104 F) and under an intense blue sky studded with equally intense white clouds, we detoured on our return trip from the gorge to this mysterious formation.

It wasn't a detour we undertook lightly. The road into the gorge is known for its combination of corrugations and razor-sharp stones and was the reason we left the caravan back at Georgetown, 84 kms (52 mls) away. It turned out to be a wise decision. Despite creeping along on the worst stretches (in our hefty 4x4) at 40 kms (24 mls) an hour, we suffered two punctures after leaving the blow. The first one destroyed the side of a back tyre but luckily the second only inflicted a slow leak so we made it back to Georgetown before the tyre deflated.

Another traveler stopped to help us change the back tyre, a difficult process given its heft and the heat, and revealed he'd begun his journey to the gorge pulling a boat trailer, suffered two punctures, and taken the whole lot back to Georgetown, before setting out again (and helping us).

In the Deep Fantasy exploration of *The White Stag* I noted how rare and/or unusual animals attract attention, and in my book *Journey: Seeking the Sacred, Spirit and Soul in the Australian Wilderness*, I discussed similar effects triggered by geological formations like Uluru and Kata Tjuta, and of the lesser known ones at Wudinna and Minnipa (described *In the Company of Birds: Poems from an Outback Odyssey*).

It's difficult to say why particular geological formations are deemed sacred. It might be their rarity, or size, or site, or prominence, or nearness to some event that unfolded close by. Regardless, sacred stones like any sacred site (gorges, pools, ruins, cathedrals and so on), are best experienced in silence which generally means attempting to visit them alone.

My first encounter with Stone Henge (in England) was on a grey winter's evening with a wind that kept others away and in an era when visitors could place their hands on the stone where Celts, Angles, Saxons, Jutes, Romans, Danes, Normans and countless others through history had once placed theirs. The experience was profound and in stark contrast to later visits where I trudged around the henge's roped off perimeter with hundreds of chattering, selfie-taking tourists. Likewise, walks around Uluru and through the magical Valley of the Winds at Kata Tjuta quickly shift from the mystical to the mundane when the voices of others intrude, and so I was relieved (and surprised) when we pulled into an empty parking area.

The Quartz Blow is promoted as a sunset viewing site which might explain the lack of daytime popularity but the fractured mound of shining stone was spectacular under the brilliant sunny sky and my husband set off with his camera. I simply stood and stared, swamped by a feeling I'd experienced at Lake Ballard, in Western Australia (described in *Journey: Seeking the Sacred, Spirit and Soul in the Australian Wilderness*). Lake Ballard is known for its Antony Gormley installation of 51, rust-red human sculptures, spread over the 16 sq kms (6 sq mls) of the lake's saltpan. The sculptures are arresting but when we set up camp in the adjacent blood-red sand hills in 2019, my attention was captured by a small, steep-sided, conical hill.

That's the real god, I thought to myself, *and the sculptures a distraction to hide the fact*, and as I stared at the Quartz Blow, I sensed the shining white and clear quartz was also a distraction, in this case, from the blow's darker and more powerful heart. I also sensed the quartz might attract things that the blow's darker heart would refuse to release.

I travel extensively both in Australia and overseas and seek out cemeteries and graveyards wherever I go. I like their silence and stillness and stories. Some, like Pere Lachaise in Paris and Highgate in London, are akin to entering another world full of beautiful statuary, mature trees, and bird song. Others, like the cemeteries of Outback Australia, are isolated, sparse, and windswept. *Their* stories are of children lost to measles; young women to tuberculosis and childbirth; and young men to waterholes and flooded rivers. And, as I stared at the Quartz Blow, it came to me that some of those drowned young men had ended up here.

The story's protagonist is representative of many young men who are (psychologically) ready to move onto their next life stage but who, unlike their friends, are directionless until they enter the water (a metaphor for the unconscious). Here in the liminal, they 'die to their old selves', and must do the work necessary to attain their new selves. There is no going back, only going forward but to do so, this particular young man must confront and assimilate his Shadow.

He correctly identifies the blow as a *she* (his anima) but there are impediments to him assimilating it which he must overcome to achieve his next life stage. He must discard his view that the fathering/nurturing demonstrated by the crows, dingoes, and kangaroos is a form of entrapment, and conquer his fear of quitting the She's shining, light-filled peak (representing consciousness/Logos) in favour of the darkness (representing the unconsciousness/Eros).

The storm represents a second plunge into the liminal: *The rain's even worse, a gigantic roar that makes the blackness deeper than a moonless, starless night. It's like the water's closing over my head all over again...* and forces him to at last take action. Panic-stricken, he quits the She to seek shelter in the trees (physical life/the green and growing) and for the first time recognises the nurturing aspect of the crows, dingoes, and kangaroos which enables him to accept and assimilate the She. His anima (now part of himself) is not something to be feared, or fought, but to be protected, which is what he and the other drowned young men do, sheltering the She (and in doing so, themselves) from the storm.

Once the protagonist attains his next life stage, he is able to see the She's beauty (the beauty of his anima/himself) in both the light (consciousness) and darkness (unconsciousness) and being whole, is free to choose his own future.

GLASS-HEART

Geth pushed the hall's door open, wedged himself around it, and heaved it shut against the wind. It was stifling inside after the night's icy gales but Geth didn't remove his cloak or even shrug it free of snow. The fighting had left him short of Rangers and he must soon be out again on patrol. At least the new batch of *hollow-bellies* would gift him time to sleep later that night.

He set his bow and quiver by the door as Morgh limped forward with the list, his face ruddy from the fire. 'How many?' asked Geth, squinting at Morgh's scrawl. An Oaklander who could write was a miracle and Geth wasn't about to insult the gods by demanding one whose writing was also clear.

'Fifteen, Ceannasai, if you not be counting the glass-heart.'

'A glass-heart? Where?' he asked, his gaze already searching the hall. The hollow-bellies sat together on one of the long wooden benches, separate to his Rangers, heads bowed low over their stew. It didn't help they kept their hoods drawn but he couldn't blame them. They weren't here to make friends but to beat off hunger's wolf until the ground thawed and the forest had food again, and then they would be back to their solitary hunting. He had their service until then, but not a day longer.

'The glass-heart be at the end nearest the fire,' said Morgh.

Geth nodded. It was small, as they always were, but ate as greedily as its companions and Geth squinted at the list again. '*Hanrin, Korm, Breth, Harl, Shenroa, Desinoa,*' he murmured. They were typical Vallender names, the females marked with an *oa* ending. '*Rasin, Sethinoa, Kyth.*'

He stopped. '*Kyth?*'

'Aye, Ceannasai. Not a Vallender, that one. She be from the Crags. She sits with the glass-heart, at the end, nearest the fire,' added Morgh needlessly.

Geth resisted the urge to storm over and tear back her hood. It had to be some other *Kyth*, he told himself, though the name wasn't common. He forced himself to read to the end of the list, shut his eyes to memorize it, and handed it back. 'Burn it,' he ordered.

'Aye, Ceannasai.'

Lists were dangerous things since the Tallon had arrived. Find your name on a list and you could find yourself on the end of a rope, or your head on a stake while the rest of you fed the crows. Geth kept no lists except in his memory. His Rangers; each new batch of hollow-bellies; those in the cots and hovels; those to be trusted; those to be dispatched back to the Tallon's gods.

His list of friends grew thin sometimes, with names torn from this world and thrust into the next, but there was a place in his mind where their smiles lived on, and their loyalty, and the bond that bound them to a cause he hoped would soon keep his lists intact.

Meanwhile he had a fresh lot of hollow-bellies to make *useful* and a *Kyth* he hoped was a stranger like the rest. He went to where his Rangers ate and waved them back as they rose from their seats.

Twenty-two enjoyed the hall's warmth, while another seven patrolled outside. Three days ago there had been thirty-three to patrol, to eat the stewed hare and turnip, and to mop its glistening sauces up with chunks of rough-ground bread.

He moved along the bench to where Alsinth sat and put his hand on her shoulder. 'A hollow-belly patrols with me tonight. You are to rest.'

'I am well, Ceannasai,' she protested. 'I have no need—'

'An order,' said Geth briefly, and moved on.

Alsinth's wound healed well, thanks to Arn, but wounds needed food and sleep to keep their bearer with the living. He flicked his head to Morgh and took up position at the head of the hollow-bellies' bench.

The rise and fall of their spoons continued uninterrupted and if they noticed him they gave no sign. 'You be listening now,' bellowed Morgh, and spoons paused as hooded-heads turned in his direction. Hoods made it hard to see faces and the bony hands that gripped the spoons were attached to similarly bony wrists except for the glass-heart. Its hand and wrist were round as acorns.

Part-stone, part-moss, the glass-heart dies but knows no loss. Geth watched it lick its spoon. He doubted the truth of the Vallender saying. Glass-heart's hungered like everyone else.

'This be your Ceannasai,' bawled Morgh, despite having the hollow-bellies' attention. 'It be him you swore your oath to serve until the quickthorn flowers, or you be taken back by your gods.'

'My name is Geth,' said Geth. 'Your oath binds you to me until winter's end. A band fights together, not alone. Until then, you are bound by my orders. You will have food, and warmth, and care for your wounds, but break your oath, and you will not have another dawn.' He paused but the shadowed faces regarded him in silence. 'Your service begins this night. Shenroa and Kyth will patrol. Morgh here will assign your other duties.'

He went to the door and reclaimed his bow and quiver. *Other duties* included scrubbing the kitchen, scraping the next meal's roots, and digging latrines. Testing their arrow, knife and sword skills must wait until the morrow, and if

72

they were like other hollow-bellies, their knife skills would be good, their arrow skills sparse, and their sword skills poor.

Hollow-bellies hunted alone, their strength in the silence of their approach and the speed of their departure. More than one Tallon had turned to find his comrade dead beside him without even a print to show the killer's trail. It fed the Tallon's belief in the land's sinister spirits, which suited Geth. Let them jump at shadows while his Rangers passed unnoticed beneath their noses.

The two hollow-bellies joined him at the door *and* the glass-heart but he quelled the impulse to order it back. Glass-hearts were as loyal as dogs to those they followed and as smart as foxes at saving their own skins. It wouldn't be near when the fighting came, only when it was over, assuming its hollow-belly master survived.

The winds had eased and the snow now fell as gently as hawthorn blossom in the Crags but the night remained icy. 'Enan!' he called.

A Ranger emerged from the trees, came to him, and nodded. 'Ceannasai?'

'This is Shenroa. Teach her your patrol.'

'Yes, Ceannasai.'

The two moved off and Geth turned back to Kyth. The hall's windows were shuttered against the night and the throw of candle-light poor. 'Take off your hood,' he ordered. She pulled it back but her face remained in shadow. '*It is you*, isn't it?' he demanded.

'I am Kyth, Ceannasai'

The same voice! Gods of ice and stone! 'Why are you here?'

'I swore an oath, Ceannasai.'

Her voice was as empty as the Crags' torched villages which made her presence worse. *Kyth*, Nyar's younger sister, whose recklessness matched her brother's as they three raced each other through the Crags' high places. *Kyth*, who had taunted and challenged him, then looked on him with different eyes and different wants, and raged when he had refused her.

The hall's western boundary remained unprotected and he set an arrow. 'We patrol,' he said curtly and set off through the oaks but she moved so quietly he glanced behind to check she followed. The hollow-bellies had taught her well or else the glass-heart had. 'Walk beside me,' he snapped, and she came level, the glass-heart at her heels.

'What do you call it?' he asked, gesturing over his shoulder.

'Wren.'

'Is that its name?'

'It's what I call her.'

It wasn't an answer but Geth didn't care. The only answer he cared about was why Kyth wasn't in the north where he had promised Nyar she would stay, safe from the slaughter that had claimed Nyar's life.

'You shouldn't be here,' he said.

'You ordered me to patrol, Ceannasai.'

He rounded on her angrily. 'Don't play the fool with me, Kyth!'

'Do you have new orders, Ceannasai?'

The air moved and he swung his bow high as a screech-owl arced, wraith-like, through the oaks. The snow stretched away in every direction, unmarked by prints, but the night was thick, and he strained his ears.

'Wolf,' the glass-heart slurred, making him jump. *They speak as slow as melting snow.* The description was apt, he concluded irritably.

'It isn't near,' said Kyth. 'Wren hears things from afar.'

'Useful,' muttered Geth, as they went on. 'Where did you find it?'

'She found me.'

'When?' asked Geth.

'Two winters ago.'

The time of Nyar's death. 'You should have stayed in the Crags. Your skills saved many lives.'

'The Tallon are no longer there.'

If the gods smiled on his plans, soon the Tallon wouldn't be *anywhere*. 'Many can kill but few can heal,' he said, as they went on. The land steepened and as snow filled the hollows, the glass-heart floundered and Kyth hauled it free.

'You should have left it where you found it,' said Geth. 'It risks you.'

'She saved me.'

'Had you stayed in the Crags, you wouldn't have needed saving!' He stopped under an oak as he fought to quell his anger. Snow thatched a squirrel's drey and clad the oak's ridged trunk in brilliant stripes of white. 'I promised Nyar you would stay in the Crags.'

'And he promised me he would live to return. It is unwise to make promises you can't keep, Ceannasai.'

'If I ordered you back to the Crags, you would have to go. You have sworn an oath.'

'And if I refused to go, you would have to kill me for the breaking of it.'

'Gods of ice and stone,' he muttered, and kicked at the snow. 'How have you lived since you left?'

'As a Vallender.'

'And how did you learn to do that?'

'Hunger is a good teacher, Ceannasai, as is hate.'

Geth glared at the oak's snowy branches. Nyar was gone and he wasn't about to lose Kyth as well. Despite her claim of Vallender skills, she was a Cragswoman, and her place wasn't here. The glass-heart's hooded eyes regarded him unblinkingly. It looked more crow than wren. 'And *it*?' he demanded, gesturing at the glass-heart. 'What did *it* teach you?'

'That death is a beginning as well as an end.'

'Nyar won't be walking the Crags again,' he said brutally.

'Bear,' slurred the glass-heart.

'It must have *excellent* hearing,' sneered Geth. 'There are no dens in this valley.'

'Bears aren't the only creatures that crawl into holes and turn their backs on the world.'

'I am *not* having you in my band, oath or no oath!'

'Give me what I want and I will go.'

The emptiness had left her voice but it only added to his anger. '*Nothing* has changed on that score.'

'Everything has changed. I am older and Nyar is dead.'

'Even more reason to honor him!'

'Cold,' slurred the glass-heart.

Geth ground his teeth as he sensed it spoke of him but Kyth pulled it into her arms and wrapped her cloak around them both. It looked as if she cradled a child and Geth turned away. He had yet to get a clear view of the glass-heart's face but it didn't matter. Glass-hearts were born wizened and died the same way though he had never seen a pillar-stone that told their names. Maybe their resting places remained unmarked, like the cots that birthed and raised them.

'You should have left it in the hall,' he said tersely.

'She stays with me.'

'Not if I order otherwise.'

'Wren swore no oath.'

'I am the *Ceannasai*,' he goaded. 'I do as I want.'

'As do the Tallon.'

The rebuke was deserved but did nothing to soothe his temper and the rest of the patrol was completed in a silence as icy as the snow.

The next morning confirmed his experience of hollow-bellies' skills, except for Kyth who was as skilled with a sword and arrow as she was with a knife. Two winters had given her plenty of time to learn, he supposed, but from whom? Hollow-bellies kept no company, even with each other.

The daylight also revealed how much Kyth had changed: her hair cropped short like a hollow-belly's and all softness gone from her face. But her eyes were the same, the deep blue of day as it turns to night. They were Nyar's eyes and they tore him apart.

He avoided her over the days that followed, which wasn't difficult given he sent the hollow-bellies on patrol with his Rangers while he dealt with the messengers who stole along the perilous ways between him and the other Ceannasai.

The last of the Tallon had withdrawn to *Crannlog*, a walled stronghold to the west. It sat atop a steep-sided knoll, bare of trees on every side. It was a predictable choice for an invader whose time in the lands was less than the seasons of *rustics* too bent to escape the pound of Tallon horses. Had the rustics lived, they might have spoken of the old ways, in the old tongue, of how Crannlog had once been thick with oak.

An oak gives succor to squirrel and boar, and when ancient with rot, to screech-owl and stoat. The hollow oaks gave their name to Crannlog too because there were more things hollow at the knoll than the trees that had long since gone.

Geth led his Rangers from the hall on a day so cold that hoar-frost mimicked blossom on the trees as if spring had come before its time. 'It be an omen,' said Morgh, as they slipped away. Geth wasn't given to Oaklander auguries but he hoped Morgh was right.

They kept to the dark-ways and went in silence, lit no fires, and ate only the oaten cakes and smoked hare they carried. Geth split the hollow-bellies between his captains who used them to scout and still the tongues of those who spied. He put Kyth with Arn, his strongest captain and the band's surgeon, and tried to think no more about her.

They reached Crannlog's bounds on the third day, and by the fourth night, the messengers confirmed the other Ceannasai were in place. They would all start the climb at moonrise, not just because the worm-ways under Crannlog held chinks to let the moonlight aid them, but because the bands must emerge as one or risk annihilation.

Geth waited with his Rangers and the hollow-bellies where bramble formed a thick and thorny door to their allocated tunnel. The stone had been carved by water then hewn by men who had known the dark-ways as well as the light, and who had feared neither.

Geth moved amongst his band, exchanging quiet words while they waited. Some he had fought with since the Tallon's foul ships had first found their shores while others had come later, when the burn of cot and kin had sent them from their valleys.

Hate drove them but hate was no shield against arrow and knife. It was fighting skills that kept them hale, and Geth ensured they had them aplenty. He needed them living, not just for their own sakes and his, but for what would come later. When the Tallon's stain had been scoured away, the destroyed must be rebuilt.

Kyth sat alone and he went to her and gazed about. 'The glass-heart's fled, has it?'

'I sent her to a place of safety. She will come to me when it is over.'

'Safety was what I wanted for you!'

'And what I wanted for Nyar.' Her eyes caught the star-sheen as she looked up at him. 'But you can't always have what you want, can you, Ceannasai?'

The climb up through Crannlog's heart was as hard as Geth had feared. Water slimed steps that seemed to go on forever but in the end, they sighted the night sky where those who kept the old tales said they would. The other bands did too. The battle was bloody as it always was when men fought for their lives, but the bands fought for the fern-filled valleys too, the deep silence of the oak forests, and the wild open places of ice and stone.

They might have shared their lands had the Tallon asked, for Vallender, Oaklander and Cragsmen had once been new here too, but the Tallon had been greedy and tried to take the lands, and by noon, the lands had been taken back.

The bands burned the Tallon corpses and fire cleansed the site as only fire can, so that Crannlog became a mighty beacon, seen from afar. Word of the victory spread, shared in raucous toasts at inns and more quietly in cots, and in the green-ways, carried on the wings of raven and crow to the deeper, darker places.

The village of Lerrig sat at Crannlog's feet and the bands took their dead and wounded there. The dead would rest for time in the nearby forests until those closest to them carried them on their final journey home, while the wounded must be salved and stitched.

A barn had been set with pallets, with warm, crackling fires and clean, hot water, to serve the needs of surgeons but the village wives came too with their herbs to quench pain and lift the spirits. Geth went to the barn to comfort his band's injured but when he saw that Kyth labored with Arn in their care, and that she was unhurt, the dread lifted from his heart and he turned his feet towards the inn.

It was time for sweetness, like the smell of quickthorn blossom after winter's lack, and he drank with those who fought and with the grey-hairs who hadn't. There were women's voices too, both old and young, and with the mead's heady fragrance came a craving for another type of sweetness.

The pretty red-head was happy to oblige *for coin* and Geth didn't begrudge her. In a world of empty fields and gutted cots, she had a need to fill her belly like everyone else. He paid and went to the room, half-expecting it to be rank with the smell of those who had used it before but it was clean and smelled of fresh straw.

It filled the mattress and rustled as he undressed and stretched out. The sheets were clean too. He had never paid coin for what a woman gave freely, though in truth, it was never free. There was trust to be handed over, and the promise of a tomorrow, but he'd been unable to promise anything since the Tallon had come, even to Kyth.

Patrols still watched the dark and he kept his weapons close although they were little recompense for the mead's sweet haze. He heard her soft step but the room was dark and he asked her name as she undressed, but she held her silence. It didn't matter. He would be gone by the morning, if not before.

She denied him her mouth but her touch was as tender as if the trade had been love, not coin, and he gave himself up to it. Years of death had left him cold but she gifted him warmth and he didn't rouse until the door opened at her leaving. For the briefest moment, candle-light illuminated her outline, short dark hair not red, and then she was gone.

The mead's sweet dregs were suddenly sour in his mouth and he cradled his head in his hands. 'Gods of ice and stone,' he groaned, and closed his eyes.

He roused again at dawn but the inn was empty of her. 'The glass-heart be sickened,' explained Morgh. 'The Cragswoman wrapped it in her cloak and put it on her shoulder like a wanderer's pack. Will you be hunting her?'

'I ordered the Cragswoman from my band,' said Geth shortly, *although that had been weeks ago.* 'She is no oath-breaker,' he added. 'Did she say where it was she went?'

'She be silent, Ceannasai, like the glass-heart. She just took up her burden and left.'

Geth passed command to Arn though there was little to do beyond the hunting of stray Tallon, who ran as hares did but as ragged as the forests' frosted leaves. Winter's embrace would finish most and the hollow-bellies the rest. Geth gave leave to his band members who must do as he did and bury those closest to them, or reclaim them from an older death to take them home.

The box Geth chose from the ossurai was of pine and unpatterned. The ossurai urged Geth to wait so he might ornament it, but Geth had waited long enough to hold Nyar again and he made the trade and headed north. Habit had him choose camps with stone at their back or groves where crows slept lightly, and when snares took squirrel, marten or hare, he cooked them in the light, doused the fire, and slept elsewhere.

His feet followed the bitter path that had brought him south after Nyar's death and by track-way and the ways of vale and ridge, he came to the pines by the stream where Nyar rested. Geth had used stone to guard him from fox and stoat, for Nyar must have sunlight, wintry though it was, and the pines' soft breeze, to free his bones from flesh for the final journey.

The breeze still blew as Geth eased the bones from rotting cloth and leather, bore them to the stream, and washed them in the water's bright rush. The pines sang as he gathered their needles, brown and resinous, to line the box, and they sang as he gently placed the bones inside, secured the lid, and went on his way. Geth carried Nyar but his thoughts were on Kyth and he wondered whether, somewhere else, her bones waited to be carried too.

Signs of the fighting were everywhere: fields uncropped, sheep free of a shepherd's hand, cots abandoned or burned, but there were new buildings too with wood raw from its cutting, and in sheltered pockets, gorse budded and snow-drops bloomed. There would be no flowers in the Crags for winter lingered longest there, but there were other compensations. When he finally trod familiar ways, he saw the Crags' ice-edged streams had lost none of their beauty, that golden eagles still ruled the daytime skies, and that firedrakes carved passages through the stars as they had since times unremembered.

And then he was home, welcomed by the embrace of many arms, given a place at any table he chose, and always a warm place to lay his head. Those who had fought or fled, slowly made their way back and while the sound of hammering and sawing filled the days, the nights were quiet. It was too soon for song, but the Cragsmen and women had always sung, and would sing again.

Geth lay Nyar to rest nearest the graveyard's pines and set a pillar-stone, though it remained unmarked. There were many pillar-stones yet to be graven, for the mason had died early in the fighting and his apprentice struggled with a workload that would have tested even his master. It didn't matter; those who loved Nyar knew where to find him.

Geth went there each evening after his labours, even when chill winds brought the last of the winter's snow. He listened to the pines, and hoped Nyar listened too, but mostly he hoped the day would come when one of those who visited their dead would turn, and it would be Kyth.

The days slipped past and the weeks, and then, in an evening fragrant with spring's first softening, he saw that someone stood in his place near the pines. They were cloaked and hooded but his heart sang. He came to her side, but she remained intent on the pillar-stone. 'How did you know Nyar was here?' he asked.

'He isn't here, only his bones.'

She didn't look at him but her hands were clasped over the small bulge of her belly and his blood ran cold as understanding dawned. 'It's mine, isn't it?' he said hoarsely.

'Yes.'

'What was it, Kyth? Revenge? I wouldn't take you, so you took me instead?' She kept her gaze on the stone, her profile so like Nyar's he winced. 'Where is the glass-heart,' he asked savagely. 'Deserted you, has it, as you deserted the band?'

'You wished me gone and I granted your wish.'

'After you took what I wouldn't give!'

'I had to save Nyar.'

'Save him? He is dead, Kyth!'

'Do you know why glass-hearts are named so, Geth?'

'Because they are brittle inside and out?' he replied sneeringly.

She reached into her cloak and carefully opened her hand to reveal a perfect sphere of glass, bright despite the evening light. 'Because in death, they look like this.'

Geth stared at her incredulously. 'Are you telling me that is a glass-heart corpse?'

Her hand closed over it protectively and it disappeared back inside her cloak. 'They are not like you and I, though they resemble us. When Wren found me I was intent on death. Nyar was gone and you had turned away. She held me that night and Nyar spoke to me.'

'It was a dream, Kyth, nothing more!'

'He told me how he died.'

'And how did he die?' demanded Geth.

'You and he scouted ahead of the band. Night was drawing on and you looked for a camp. There was a stream and pines but the vale was narrow and you distrusted it. But Nyar liked to sleep to the sound of water and the pines meant there were martens to trap. You argued but Nyar was stubborn and when you turned back to where the band waited, he lingered. The arrow took him in the throat. He was dead before you reached him.'

'How do you know this?' choked Geth. 'No one was there!'

'Nyar told me. You cradled him in your arms by the stream so he could hear its music and buried him there amongst the pines so he could hear theirs. You didn't return to the band until night but Nyar had gone by then.'

'You can't know this!' cried Geth.

'The dead seek those they love but you and I were too far apart,' continued Kyth quietly. 'The darkness took him and there he might have stayed had not Wren saved him and then saved me. But a soul is a mighty burden to carry and Wren sickened, as glass-hearts always do. Their lives are short so those we love can live on.'

She looked at Geth for the first time. 'I had to give Nyar a way back to us. I have always loved you, Geth, but you were right to refuse me when I was young in head and heart and full of my own needs. It has been a hard learning for me to be other. What I have done, I have done for Nyar, and for you who loved him, but also for myself who loves you both.'

Geth took a shuddering breath. 'You claim our child is Nyar?'

'Our child is itself but carries Nyar's spirit. That is the gift Wren gave me, the gift all glass-hearts give.'

'And what did you give it?' he demanded, angered again. 'What did *you* trade for the glass-heart's *generosity*?'

'A human touch and human kindness, and a promise to keep her safe in death, as you kept Nyar safe in death.'

'But not in life,' said Geth raggedly.

'Neither of us could. Not the last time.'

'And this time?'

'That is for you to choose. My choices are made.'

She walked back towards where others gathered, warmed by their fires under shingle and thatch, but Geth stayed where he was. The child had been made with love, whether he believed Kyth's tale or not, and whether his part had been willing or not. He had craved something that night at the inn, that wasn't cold death, and Kyth had gifted it. And now they were back in the Crags: he and Kyth, Nyar and the one yet to be born who, one way or another, was part of them all.

The way ahead should be clear but he loitered. The night was still and the pines silent, and then a firedrake lit the sky, brilliant for a moment, before the dark reclaimed it. A smaller light spilled from the cots but a warmer one, and he turned his feet that way, the way Kyth had already gone.

Glass-Heart Deep Fantasy Retelling

My fantasy brain sometimes wonders whether the loss of our broader kin is responsible for our fascination with the human-like species such as elves, dwarves, trolls, goblins, pixies, brownies and so on found in myth, fantasy, and folklore. At various times on the planet, there have been at least eight other species of humans (hominins) apart from us (Homo Sapiens), and our DNA reveals we interbred with at least two of them (Denisovans and Neanderthals) and yet here we are today, apparently alone.

While I've written about angels and part angels (*Angel Caste* series), elf-like beings (*The Emerald Serpent*), and shape-shifters (*I Heard the Wolf Call My Name*) as part of my fantasy works, I also wonder whether the loss of human variation is a matter of definition rather than actuality, and whether different versions of humans do exist but are disguised by the various labels applied to them.

Is someone labeled intersex a flawed (lesser) version of a male or female or something else entirely? And if someone sees colour differently from the majority, do they suffer from monochromatism, dichromatism or anomalous trichromatism, or simply have a unique view of the world? One group with a very obvious difference are people born with an extra chromosome in some or all their cells, a state known as Down Syndrome.

While Down Syndrome can also produce a range of serious health conditions, those with Down Syndrome don't seem to figure prominently in crimes committed by 'normal people' such as theft, rape, and murder. However, this is merely an observation arising from my musings.

I'm neither a criminologist nor medical practitioner.

While readers might not recognise Wren has Down Syndrome in *Glass-Heart*, I've written about the condition more obviously in *The Dragon of the Drowned World*. In that story, we get to know the character with Down Syndrome (Davy) through the loving memories of his brother Jojo. As a happy and affectionate but developmentally delayed child, Davy doesn't challenge any stereotypes but his mother does when she says Davy's lack of worry suggests he has the *right* number of chromosomes (and the worriers in the family too few).

In Glass-Heart, Wren's physical appearance and slurred speech are viewed sneeringly and her label of glass-heart implies a subhuman frailty, but she is far more than she appears. In a Deep Fantasy reading of the story, Wren helps Kyth in her transition to her next life stage in the same way the seven dwarves help Snow White, the birds help Cinderella (when they separate lentils from coals), and the ants help Psyche (in the myth of Pysche and Eros) when they sort a massive pile of mixed seeds (an impossible task set by Eros's mother).

Kyth is in the liminal (the two years between leaving the Crags and reconnecting with Geth before the battle of Crannlog) and in crisis when she comes across Wren. In Campbell's hero journey, this is often when the Helper appears. As Kyth later tells Geth: *When Wren found me I was intent on death. Nyar was gone and you had turned away*. In those two years, Kyth learns to live alone and to kill, thus her animus/Logos become dominant over her anima/Eros. In order to move onto her next life-stage, she needs to assimilate these two aspect of her psyche. She does so by taking on the mothering/caring/protection of Wren and, by extension, of her dead brother's soul.

Her new life stage (integration of anima and animus) allows her to recognise her earlier want of Geth as immature and selfish, and to take Geth in love anonymously and selflessly. In Geth's own words:... *her touch was as tender as if the trade had been love, not coin ... Years of death had left him cold but she gifted him warmth* ... Her new life stage also allows her to return to healing (after the battle at Crannlog), continue to protect Wren in death, and keep her brother's soul safe.

Geth's time in the liminal is also long and he doesn't assume his next life stage until he chooses to follow Kyth away from the desolation of Nyar's grave to the warmth and connection of the cots. Geth's animus is very much in the ascendant, shored up and augmented by his close, boyhood friendship with Nyar, his later adult one, and by the fighting.

He leaves his old life (and Kyth, his anima) behind at the Crags and his reaction to Kyth's appearance before the final battle is anger and rejection, more for Nyar's sake than Kyth's. He again refuses her advances, although this time (unbeknownst to him) Kyth seeks to save Nyar's soul:

> *'Give me what I want and I will go.'*
> *The emptiness had left her voice but it only added to his (Geth's) anger.*
> *'Nothing has changed on that score.'*
> *'Everything has changed. I am older and Nyar is dead.'*
> *'Even more reason to honor him!'*

Geth goes through a drawn-out process to bring his animus back to a state receptive of his anima (as represented by Kyth). After the final battle, he craves the *warmth* (connection/anima) that sexual love offers, but seeks to control the exchange by buying sex, rather than opening himself to what

Kyth offers. He must then complete a series of ritualised actions to separate himself from his disproportionate animus (represented by Nyar). He cleans the clothing and flesh from Nyar's bones, boxes them up, takes them back to the Crags, and buries them. But even as he carries them, he thinks of Kyth, as he does when he keeps vigil at Nyar's graveside.

Even so, it doesn't take much to rouse his anger again (his animus to reassert itself) when Kyth appears and he needs a second ritualised separation from Nyar, which Kyth delivers by taking Geth step by step through Nyar's death. Geth still lingers near Nyar after Kyth walks away and it is the appearance of the firedrake/ dragon (dragons are associated with the earth's *creative* energies) that finally integrates his anima and animus, delivers him his next life stage, and allows him to follow.

So, what of Nyar who enters the liminal after his physical death and continues in the liminal in Wren's keeping and, after Wren's physical death, as part of Kyth's unborn child? While we don't learn how Nyar will manifest when the child is born, or how different he will be from his previous life (stage), the story suggests reincarnation, that is, a return in a new life stage.

We don't know of Wren's life before her meeting with Kyth or afterwards and it is unclear whether the shining globe is both Wren's physical and spiritual remains, or just one or the other. Being in Kyth's safe-keeping suggests a liminal state from which Wren will emerge. I'm intending to write more about glass-hearts in my next series, so (as a Pantser) I'll discover more then.

GHOST STREAM

Will's Story

The lettering on my tombstone is so weathered it's hard to read but I don't need to. I know I'm Will Davis, second son of Lord Greyland, beloved brother of George and Arabella, taken by the water at 24. Arabella is dead too like George, but they grew old and are at peace now while I still linger.

I came to this scorched, alien land because Johnny wanted to, or more correctly, needed to come, to make his fortune. I could have stayed at home in comfort but Johnny was more like a brother to me than George ever was. Being the second son of a lord granted me a life of ease on grand estates, but no claim to them, unlike George who entered the world first. It was George who inherited our father's title and duty to enrich and safeguard our estates as our forebears had. My darling sister Arabella had a duty too which was to marry well to add to our estates, but as a second-born son, my estates must be found elsewhere.

Johnny's decision to leave made mine easier. He was the son of one of our foresters and had little to commend him beyond his father's excellent character but his lack troubled him less than mine troubled me perhaps because, in choosing to leave, he had nothing to lose. 'A fortune can be made in wool or beef,' he said, 'and being your own man is beyond the measure of riches.'

I thought Father would forbid my plan to go adventuring or that Arabella would for we were close, as twins mainly are. It was a closeness that alerted me to her being swept away on a seaside jaunt but Arabella seemed as keen as father to wave me off on the good ship Siren, though I knew her well enough to see the sadness in her face. There was something else there too, relief perhaps, that our long preparations had drawn to an end.

I had little to do with the seas before Arabella's near drowning, unlike Father, who had sailed upon them in noble service and carried the very roar of the oceans in his veins. As a seaman, he had cheated Death more than once and I hoped to do the same, for I knew from his tales the ocean exacted a price for those who escaped its thrall.

The voyage was long with its fair share of storms and it was then his words returned to haunt me. Johnny remained undaunted and I somehow found the courage to stand beside him on the rain-lashed deck and shout our contempt for the ocean's pounding squalls. There were brilliant sunny days too when the waters hid their malice beneath shining greens and blues, and by the time we arrived at the ramshackle port, Johnny's excitement and hope had become my excitement and hope as well.

Father assigned me funds enough to take up two runs, the second for Johnny to manage, and to purchase the cattle whose meat would build our fortunes. The natives caused no trouble, having been dispersed before we arrived. There was feed enough for our cattle and water, *when it rained*, but it rained little in that first year despite the broad streambeds that told me heavy rains had fallen and, we hoped, would fall again.

The natives were happy to work for their rations and made decent stockmen, seeming to know the nature of both horse and steer, as they knew the natures of the strange creatures that bounded and burrowed. I worked with a native I called Billy, given his native name was indecipherable, and he called me Boss. He spoke little and with the strange slur the natives used in their attempts at English, but we got along well enough.

There was little time for talk anyway with fences to build, *and* sheds to house our equipment and stores, *and* huts for me and the men who came in search of work. It was a stony land and as time went on we built stone houses much superior to those early huts but rude even compared to the tenants' cots on the estates back home.

The work was hard but times were good around the fire each night with Johnny and the men we came to trust. Rain would have added to our cheer, but the wells we dug were sufficient in those early months and the stock we raised gave us funds to grow our herds. I had few letters from my father and none from George, but many from Arabella who promised to visit once she had settled into her role of wife and mother on her husband's estates adjacent to ours. I knew it would be years before I saw her again but I was content she not risk the seas as I had. Few months passed without some tale of catastrophe, for the coasts of this new land were edged with soaring cliffs that dashed ships to pieces along with their hapless passengers and crews.

Being an island, the lands had salt water aplenty, but lacked the sweet water we must have if our endeavour were not to fail. The wells sank lower but there was a good freshwater spring a little ways off we could use, *if* we built channels to deliver it to our runs. The task would be hard and long but that was not the only reason I delayed.

Billy was shy like the other natives and always addressed me with down cast eyes cast but they flashed to mine when I mentioned my plan to divert the spring water. 'Special place, Boss. No go there.'

Natives are superstitious but I had never seen anger in Billy before or in the other natives who lined up for their rations. There were runs where the natives had walked off due to some perceived slight or other and I did not want that kind of trouble here. I needed them to keep our enterprise growing and I knew from Father's estates that happy men worked better than disgruntled ones.

But no rain fell and the time came when we must have water or our cattle perish and so the work began. No native would bend his back with a shovel so it was those straight from the ships who started the digging. I ignored Billy's sullen disapproval but soon after we started, I noticed the native women and children had disappeared.

'Where your women?' I asked him.

'Gone away,' he muttered. 'This bad place now. Water angry.'It rained that day, a mighty deluge that swept across the ground and I wished I had made the water angry earlier. The rain did not last and the next morning the ground was again as dry as dust but that night I was woken by a roar. Worse still, was the pound of hoofs that told me the cattle ran in panic. The night was thick as I headed out with the stockmen, Billy by my side, to discover the river I had never seen flow, stormed along in full flood. I rode with the men to save the cattle but the water cut between us so that only Billy was with me as we drove the cattle back and then the water divided us too. I heard Billy's shout as I spurred after some breakaways and then my horse was gone, and I was in the torrent, and the night turned in upon itself. And now I linger here, dead but not at peace, when all I want is rest.

Billy's Story

Auntie Annie says I can tell Billy's story. 'E passed away long time ago, but Auntie Annie wants people to know, to keep safe, black fella *and* white fella. Auntie says I can talk about 'im because *Billy* was just a name given by the white fellas, like they give their dogs and 'orses names. Some of Billy's story is missin' and some not for white fella ears but Billy knew, like all black fellas, the creation spirits made us and all the lands 'ere about, and that there're still 'ere, sleepin' in special places like caves and mountains and springs.

Billy knew the spring was a sleepin' place and told the white fellas stay away but the white fellas too impatient. Rain knows nothin' about time. It comes when it's ready, Auntie Annie says. The white fellas see the rain would come again because the riverbeds are full of stones rolled smooth by water. Billy said the white fellas called 'em ghost streams, as if they were dead, but Auntie Annie says water's never dead. After rain, the sky lifts it back up again to stop the land from floodin' and the sky from growin' parched. The water goes back and forth, she says, in a givin' and takin'.

Well, the white fella got 'is water all right, but the water got 'im. A givin' and takin', just as Auntie Annie said. There's a price for disturbin' the spirit's sleep, and even in death, the white fella gets no peace.

Arabella's Story I

The day I almost drowned is graven in my mind, but not for the reasons you might think. Indeed, while the horrid sense of suffocation remains with me to this day, it was Father's words that evening, after Nanny had soothed my whimpers, that shocked me most.

I rarely entered Father's rooms where he wrote at his big mahogany desk, or met with stern, sea-weathered men to chink glasses of claret and leave the room filled with the nutty smell of tobacco.

The fire flames glowed on the leather seat Father directed me to and then, surprisingly, Johnny came in and stood in front of the fire, hands clasped behind his back like a younger version Father.

Johnny was Will's friend and like Will, was kind to me, despite being busy helping Will oversee the workers or accompanying Will on hunts through our parks and forests. He was sombre, which was so unlike him I stared and only looked at Father when his resonant voice intruded.

At first I thought Father told me a story, for his tale seemed to be of others, of *their* adventures and fates, but then I came to understand he spoke of our forebears whose lives had been taken by pond, river or stream, or whose bones were still tossed by mighty oceans; and of those who had escaped a watery death, and the price that one day, someone else had paid.

Horror descended upon me as the story of my family line unfolded and I understood the water had tried to claim me this day, in recompense for some earlier debt Father hinted was his, for he had swum to safety from the wreckage of horrendous sea battles more than once. Whatever the truth, my rescue that day by Will had increased the debt and the water's vengeful want for payment.

I learned the threat was deadliest on our estates where we should have been safest; where we knew every nook in every forest and park and where those of our line stared down at us from the Great Hall's gallery. I had thought little about the men bedecked in wealth and power and the women clad in bejewelled finery, but now I learned Sir Wilfred's infant son had drowned when apoplexy had seized his nurse while bathing him; that Great Uncle Buckland's daughter had been taken to her grave by water-filled lungs; that Cousin Edward and his new bride had plunged to their deaths when the bridge over the Grey Stream collapsed under their carriage. Others had been crushed by trees toppled by rain-sodden ground, slipped from the Hall's rain-slicked roof, or gone boating on the Frogging Pond and not returned.

The risk was greatest to those who thwarted the water's intent, Father said, and so Will would be safer far from us in a place renowned for its *lack* of water. Johnny would protect him on the voyage and in the new lands where they would build a future together.

My heart was broken by the impending loss of Will and his friend, who I counted as my friend as well, but I felt a surge of gratitude for the sacrifice Johnny made to keep my brother safe. It comforted me to know that if I must lose Will, he would be with someone who loved him too.

Johnny's Story

It's a hard thing to be a bastard but I was luckier than most for while Lord Greyland never acknowledged me publicly *or* privately, his favour granted me almost as many opportunities as his second-born son. Neither of us could look forward to the trappings of those with more fortunate births but my life had turned out well enough *until* the Lady Arabella's brush with death.

Lord Greyland had hinted at the risk water posed to his line while I was still a boy. The *family curse*, he called it and had instructed me to spend time with Will both as friend and guardian, although the latter was never explicit until the Lady Arabella's near drowning. Even so, I was well aware the life I enjoyed was bound up with Will's welfare and so took my responsibilities very seriously.

Being Will's friend was no hardship at all, for he was honest and open-hearted, and nor was the guardianship, for Will was no more reckless than any other man his age. I made sure our hunts avoided the estates' ponds and streams, and to be with him on any excursion to the Frogging Pond. But my status meant I wasn't in Lord Greyland's party when Will thwarted the ocean's attempt to claim the Lady Arabella's life.

As Lord Greyland later told me, Will's heroism had likely sealed his fate *if* he remained at the estates and so leave he must and, as his guardian, I must leave too. The notion of making my fortune in a new land excited me, for Lord Greyland's favour would cease with his death, and

George wouldn't honour the relationship, even if he knew of it, which I suspected he didn't.

And so preparations for the journey were made, our farewells delivered, and we departed. Storms battered our brave little ship so badly I feared the sea would claim Will anyway and the rest of the Siren's souls, passengers and crew alike. I countered my fears with defiance, determined not to go to my death meekly, but we arrived in the hot brown land safely and took up our runs.

Water was scarce, which suited my guarding duties, and the wells we dug were fenced for safety, so my concerns ebbed over the months. I couldn't be with Will all the time anyway because I had a run to manage.

The first year passed in hard labour under scorching skies but it was a good life made better by knowing I built my fortune. Will's plan to divert water from the spring made me uneasy but no man could argue against it, myself included, for when clouds refuse to send water, it must be sourced elsewhere or our labours be in vain, as my guardianship ultimately proved to be.

Not that Lord Greyland attributed any blame to me. Will had been in the ground less than six months when the Lord's letter arrived to acknowledge Will's death and assign me ownership of both runs on condition I did not return. And I was happy to oblige given the other matters the Lord's letter contained.

Arabella's Story II

The news I had long dreaded arrived one bleak winter's morning. Will was gone, claimed by the water like so many of our line before him. Sending him to the far side of the world had not saved him. Missing his laughing face and my children missing the joy of their uncle's presence had all been in vain.

In the dark months that followed, I yearned to go to him, to stand where the roaring waters had snatched him away and call his name as if he lingered and could hear me. Part of me knew it was impossible. The children were too young to leave and the risk of crossing the oceans was suddenly very real, but I dreamed of him often, as if his spirit called to mine, and I feared he was not at peace at all.

It was my dear father who, knowing of our closeness and my distress, suggested the tombstone. It would be hewn from the quarries on our estates and inscribed with the words I hoped never to utter, so that Will's resting place would be marked with both a part of his home and a part of my heart. Father kept me informed of the stone's progress over the oceans, of its landing at the port where Will and Johnny had landed just a few years earlier, of its overland trip by bullock train, and of its setting in place. The stone would keep him safe, I comforted myself, even from the water.

Lord Greyland's Story

War is a series of trades: advance and retreat, truth and deceit. There is nothing noble about it. My estates were born from such trades and prosper because of them but no trade signe appears on our coat of arms and nor have I spoken of them even to George. I will leave letters to ensure he understands the full breadth of his responsibilities, as my father left letters for me.

Johnny knows more than George, for I must be more open with my bastard to keep the estates safe and later, after Will's death, to ensure Johnny stays far away along with any residual debt. Johnny has done well enough from my arrangements and even were he to return, the words of bastard mean nothing.

My forebears include many who served king and country at sea and like them, when I found myself deep in the ocean's merciless grip, with the last of my breath torn from my lungs, I traded the life of another in my line for my own. The first-born son must secure the estates and the daughter ensure their enlargement by marrying well, but a second-born son is expendable.

I admit to a certain fondness for Will and I tried to keep him safe *until* the ocean seized Arabella to remind me of my debt . And so I sent Will away along with the threat he posed and charged my bastard with ensuring he never returned.

The water took its payment in the end, as water always does, but the dead do not always rest easy, and when Arabella told me of Will's dream visitations, I sent a tombstone to seal him in. There must be no returning, even in spirit-form, to risk those who guard the estates of my line and of the line to come.

Ghost Stream Deep Fantasy Retelling

I first visited the Outback 1987 after a friend suggested an expedition to the Flinders Ranges in South Australia. I only had a vague idea of the Outback then that consisted of it being hot, red, and far away. We set off with a great deal of excitement in our very first 4x4 (a pre-loved short wheelbase Toyota with galloping horses along the side and a great deal of less fashionable rust), our eleven month old daughter, and a tiny camper trailer (the type with a wind up roof and pull out canvass-ceilinged beds at each end).

I grew up in north-eastern Victoria (Australia), home to the smoky blues of the Great Dividing Range, silvery inland lakes, and the deep greens of eucalypts, so when I first saw the rust-blood reds of the Outback's sands and its ancient ranges worn down to ragged nubs, they seemed as alien as Mars. But what I remember most powerfully from that first trip was the profound wonderment and joy the Outback gifted me then, and has continued to gift me on every visit since.

Yet the Outback, for all its sublime beauty, is a harsh and unforgiving place even with today's modern conveniences, and was many times more so for early European settlers, as the countless ruins they left behind testify. Earlier I noted my fascination with the stories Outback cemeteries tell and, as an ex-Geographer, my continued interest in less common features such as Quartz Blows (the subject of *Rite*), and on a recent trip to the Outback, I discovered the *ghost stream*, another feature I had never heard of.

It turned out to be a more evocative term for an intermittent stream: a stream (or river) that flows only infrequently. Ghost streams are the reason travelers are warned not to camp in or near the Outback's nice, soft, sandy, empty riverbeds. Substantial rains might only fall occasionally and many kilometres away, but it doesn't take long to arrive downstream in raging torrents (which is why flood markers on Outback roads can be several metres high).

The term ghost stream caught my attention in the same way that quartz blow did, but so did other things on that particular Outback trip. The inheritance practice of primogeniture (passing property to the first born son or nearest male relative) used by the wealthy of the UK and Europe, provided a reason for later born sons to journey to places like Australia to make their fortunes, and those that did, sometimes left behind the ruins of substantial homesteads to mark their success.

First Nations people also left their imprint on the land (and continue to), although it's often not visible to the European eye. As well, the location/significance of many of First Nation special and/or sacred sites has been lost due to the European invasion, or misidentified, or concealed for cultural reasons.

Many of the elements in *Ghost Stream* link to water which, as discussed, is a common symbol for the unconscious and it is in the unconscious that the Shadow (the repressed parts of self) must be confronted and assimilated for the next life stage to be attained. But, as the title of *Ghost Stream* suggests, the necessary 'water of change' is inconstant and so the psychological journeys of those in the story are impeded or even entirely blocked.

The aptly named Lord *Grayson* is, like his forebears, marooned in the liminal/grey between the black and white of his previous and coming life stages and again, like his forebears, he trades his future self (in the form of his second born son) for the safety of his present (moribund) state.

Lord Grayson and his estates are one and the same, and so his duty to preserve/protect them is the same as preserving/protecting his present life stage. His responsibilities, set out in the letters he received from his father and which he in turn will leave for his first born son, lock him and his heir into their static states.

His rejection of the opportunities for change/reinvigoration his unconscious presents (his near drownings/relinquishment of previous life) means he is both the perpetrator and victim of the forces that keep him as he is. When Lord Grayson says: *War is a series of trades: advance and retreat, truth and deceit. There is nothing noble about it* he might well be describing the war between his conscious and unconscious minds and his ignoble trade of his second son's future life for his own present one.

While George's life isn't explored, it is predictable he will perpetuate his father's legacy. Arabella is scarcely freer than her father and elder brother as she is also contained/controlled by her obligation to protect/enlarge the estates. Motherhood provides her with movement to the next life stage (she can't simultaneously be the nymph/virgin and the matron/mother) but any further advancement is curtailed by her duties to her (husband's) estates and children.

As she says: *I yearned to go to him* (Will – her twin brother)... but ...*The children were too young to leave and the risk of crossing the oceans was suddenly very real, but I dreamed of him often, as if his spirit called to mine, and I feared he was not at peace at all.* As previously discussed, male-female twins can represent the animus and anima of a single entity but in *Ghost Stream*, Arabella's full integration of her animus (represented by Will) is blocked by Lord Grayson. *As he says: ... when Arabella told me of Will's dream visitations, I sent a tombstone to seal him in.*

Will and Johnny have the most chance of escaping the moribund cycle perpetuated by Lord Grayson but in a sense, Johnny is as much an extension of Lord Grayson as George is and confined to his present life stage by his powerlessness as a bastard, and by the prosperity his compliance promises.

As discussed, a new life stage requires the (psychological) death of the old which can be achieved as part of a physical journey (the dual physical/psychological hero journey identified by Joseph Campbell). Will is defiant in the face of storms that threaten his physical self on the voyage but which, in a Deep Fantasy reading (where water symbolises the unconscious), provide the means for psychological change. Barriers also exist to Will accessing his unconscious when he disembarks: a lack of rainfall, fenced off wells, and the *forbidden* First Nation's spring.

The need for physical water is triggered by a physical drought, but dryness, aridity, and deserts are common metaphors for the barrenness of an exhausted life stage. This metaphor is obvious in the (chronologically) first *StarWars* film when we meet Luke Skywalker, chafing at the bit for change, but stuck in Tatooine's empty deserts.

Joseph Campbell's monomyth calls the reluctance of a hero to set out physically (and thus initiate a psychological journey of change) the *refusal of the quest*. Will comes from a long line of refusers, his father being an obvious example who, when faced with the full onslaught of his unconscious mind's demand for change (the *drowning* of his old self), sacrifices his son (symbolic of a new life stage).

Will's unconscious can only tolerate its own aridity for so long before a deluge overwhelms his conscious psychological defences. His physical drowning, symbolises the psychological death of his old self, but he remains marooned in the liminal. Full integration of his animus with his anima (represented by Arabella) might move him on, but is prevented by Lord Grayson who uses a tomb stone to 'seal him in' and so Will is doomed to replicate his father's fate.

END OF THE WHITE STAG AND OTHER STORIES WITH DEEP FANTASY RETELLINGS.

If you enjoyed delving into Deep Fantasy, you might enjoy *Journey: Seeking the Sacred, Spirit and Soul in the Australian Wilderness* and the fictional works of *The Emerald Serpent*, *Heart Hunter*, and the *Angel Caste* series.

Authors need reviews! It's how our readers find us. I would love you to leave me an honest review on Amazon, Goodreads, or another of your favourite reader sites. Here is a peek of *The Emerald Serpent*, a Deep Fantasy story set in a world composed of three planes.

Cormac called a rest break when they came to a second grove of pines. A small waterfall slid down the slope like a silver ribbon to pool briefly in a stony basin before it flowed away. They drank from it and replenished their waterskins and then Artair and Tormod settled on a nearby log. Etaine remained beside the pool, scooping the cool water over her bruised face.

The Goddess's voice sang in the water's chime but Etaine's enjoyment was ruined by Cormac's prowl up and down behind her and she closed her eyes to shut him out. In an instant she was in the wondrous landscape of the Emerald Way where emerald drifts hinted the joy of Ellair's presence might still be possible. But then Cormac's voice intruded, calling her name, and she reeled in confusion thinking that somehow he was there with her in the Emerald Way.

'Etaine?'

The Emerald Way dissipated in an instant and she was back in the Light Way where Cormac crouched beside her, his dark eyes filled with the emerald light he'd wrenched her from.

'Where is it you go?' he whispered.

'Somewhere better than here with you,' she muttered, disorientated by the violence of her return. She'd never gone so quickly into the Emerald Way nor so deeply, and she struggled to make sense of her surroundings.

All softness left Cormac's face and he stood. 'Time to leave,' he said.

Works by K S Nikakis

Non-Fiction
Travel and Poetry

Journey: Seeking the Sacred, Spirit and Soul in the Australian Wilderness – For fans of Joseph Campbell's hero journey

When we set out into the wilderness, what is it we really seek?

Do we seek new sights or do we seek new selves? And are we really on one journey or on two?

Journeying fifteen thousand kilometres into Australia's blood-red heart, Nikakis discovers that every journey is perilous, for travellers risk carrying the clutter of their outer lives with them; a clutter that blinds them to the other journey they crave; that of the inner soul-journey into a deeper understanding of self.

To enter Australia's vast Outback wilderness, is to enter a place of endless horizons; a place doused with brilliant gold dawns and dazzling sunsets; a place silvered by star-encrusted night skies and, most importantly, a place of hidden sacred places in whose deep stillness our inner journeys can at last unfold.

In the spirit of travellers like Robert Macfarlane and Scott Stillman, Nikakis asks what it is we really see, feel and understand when we follow in the steps of those who have gone before us deep into the wilderness.

Drawing on her Ph.D. in Joseph Campbell's hero myth, and using original poetry and novel extracts, Nikakis takes us on this second journey; a journey of the sacred, spirit and soul, where our inner selves finally have the time and space to gift us richer and more fully-realised lives.

In the Company of Birds - Poems from an Outback Odyssey

What do we lose when we cease to be a child and become an adult? What precious thing do we let slip away and barely notice?

Watch any child in a garden or park or wilderness area as they discover the natural world. Listen to their ooh's of delight at the sight of a caterpillar on a leaf, their excited squeals as a butterfly bobs past, their clap of hands and gap-toothed grins at the gambol of some young animal.

Children delight in the most common and mundane elements of the natural world with a pure and unsullied joy that many of us, somewhere in our journey to adulthood, have lost. We largely remain unaware of our loss, although I recall the exact moment I became conscious that while I saw the beauty of the natural world, I no longer felt it in the deepest parts of my soul.

As adults, we might continue to admire the natural world's beauty on an intellectual level and seek connection with it for our physical, mental, and spiritual health. It's one of the reasons I set out on a 50 day journey through Australia's southern wilderness, but how often do we ignore the sparrows at our feet in our eagerness to admire the eagles that soar above? And when so many things demand our adult attention, how do we even make time to look in the first place?

Beauty surrounds us, as it surrounds a child, but our adult gaze seeks out the extraordinary and so blinds us to the ordinary, denying us the visceral joy that such things deliver. To reclaim this joy, we must suspend our adult judgement and clear our gaze as a child does.

A journey in the company of birds allows us the time and space to do so. Birds require us to search the ground as well as the sky, to delight in the raven's harsh croak as well as the honeyeater's sweet song, to take pleasure in the sparrow's brown plumage as well as the fairywren's blue. And as we still, and look, and listen, we are ultimately rewarded with the return of all we've lost.

And so, let us begin this journey of rediscovery, in the company of birds.

Glastonbury – Meditations on the Goddess

What is the sacred? Where can we find it? And why do we need it?

The pure notes of dawn's first birdsong; the spark of stars into the night sky; the setting sun's fiery path across ocean waves, can all make us stop, hold our breath, and know, deep within ourselves, we are in the presence of the sacred.

For some people, the sacred is found within ornate buildings crowned with crosses, crescents or stars, spaces that bring them closer to their god. For others, the sacred resides in humbler temples or under the spreading branches of hallowed trees.

Glastonbury has long been revered as a sacred space that, like all sacred spaces, elicits a sense of something greater, grander, and infinitely more meaningful than our everyday lives.

In my wanders through Glastonbury's cobbled streets and over its rolling fields, I discovered the sacred was everywhere and often many-layered, with church built upon temple and temple built upon spring and so, in my meditations on its nature, I came to call it the Goddess, in homage to the ancient, over-arching, regenerative source of all things.

Fantasy Novel Series

Angel Caste 5 book series
Book 1 Angel Blood

Street-kid, thief, criminal: Viv is desperate to change her life.

On day release from jail to attend the funeral of her father, a violent drunk she feared and despised, her real father turns up, the powerful angel Archae Kald. He offers to reunite Viv with the mother she thought dead and, determined to find the only person who has ever loved her, Viv travels through a rift to the male angel world of Ezam.

Kald assigns his protégé, the beautiful angel Thris, to guide Viv to her mother. It is Thris's job to keep Viv safe in the Rynth, the vast tangle of worlds she never knew existed. But Viv is deeply damaged from her life on the streets and in no mood to trust anyone, even an angel with a face to die for. They set out, but as the complications multiply, disaster follows.

Thris might be eons old, but he knows little about females, especially ones who are half human. Like his closest friends, Ash and Ky, all he wants to do is transcend but when he and Viv stumble into the acrid world of Moth Fold, and Viv's latent angel traits emerge, transcendence seems the last thing possible.

After a devastating attack, Viv ends up lost and alone in the Rynth. Will she survive to continue the search for her mother? Or end her days in an alien world?

If you like your female heroes feisty, your male angels glorious, your fantasy worlds filled with brilliant landscapes and a dash of romance, you will love *Angel Blood*, Book 1 in the five book fantasy series *Angel Caste*.

Buy *Angel Blood* today to start your amazing adventure with Viv and Thris in the wild worlds of the Rynth.

Book 2 Angel Breath

Viv can survive on the streets, but can she survive in the Rynth?

Thris is gone, his exquisite body torn apart, and borne away by Ash and Ky. Viv fears she will never see him again, but there is no way she is turning back. She journeys on through the Rynth, narrowly escaping murderous landscapes and worlds full of savage creatures. Her life on the streets might have been a nightmare, but at least it taught her how to run, hide, and out-wit pursuers.

And then, when all seems lost, Thris returns. Viv is overjoyed, but her happiness is short-lived. He isn't the angel he was, and he isn't alone. Ky is with him, and Ky hates Viv. The feeling is mutual, but Ky's terror of the Rynth adds to their peril and they don't get far before they are besieged by savage, long-armed creatures. When Ky is injured, Thris is confronted with a terrible decision, and must abandon Viv to save him.

Viv journeys on but stumbles into a war zone. Desperate to escape, she is determined to take the next rift out, but finds a little girl, the sole survivor of a massacre. Recognizing the chance to make amends for the accident that landed her in jail, Viv delays the search for her mother, to take the little girl to safety.

But in an alien, war-torn world, it is all but impossible to tell friend from foe, and when the little girl falls ill, Viv must take a terrible risk. Will Viv manage to save the little girl? Or will the fighting cost them both their lives?

If you like your female heroes feisty, your male angels glorious, your fantasy worlds filled with brilliant landscapes and a dash of romance, you will love *Angel Breath*, Book 2 in the five book fantasy series *Angel Caste*.

Buy *Angel Breath* today to continue your amazing journey with Viv and Thris through the wild worlds of the Rynth.

Book 3 Angel Bone

Viv didn't abscond from jail to become someone else's prisoner, but that seems to be her fate.

As chance would have it, she resembles a people called the elddra, and that makes her both despised and desired. It also makes friends few and far between. Viv is desperate to deliver the little girl to safety, take a rift out, and resume the search for her mother, but dodging the new world's warring factions proves harder than she thinks.

As they journey on through strange and hostile lands, the little girl's trust and affection for Viv grows, and Viv is surprised by her own feelings of fierce protectiveness. And then, as they near safety, disaster strikes. They are overtaken by fighters and separated. Viv is seized and when the fighters are annihilated by a second force, their leader assumes she is one of the enemy. Prevented from executing her on the spot, the leader condemns her to a slower, more painful death.

In his own world, Thris struggles to care for Ky who is traumatized by his time in the Rynth, and when Ky flees, they end up imprisoned in a maze-like world where the only way out is a death-trap. Their hopes for rescue lie in Ash, but Ash is trapped too, entranced by a world of shining light, and unaware of his friends' plight.

Will Viv survive to be reunited with the child she loves? Or will she lose her too, as she has lost her mother and Thris?

If you like your female heroes feisty, your male angels glorious, your fantasy worlds filled with brilliant landscapes and a dash of romance, you will love *Angel Bone*, Book 3 in the five book fantasy series *Angel Caste.*

Buy *Angel Bone* today to continue your amazing journey with Viv and Thris through the wild worlds of the Rynth.

Book 4 Angel Bound

Viv thought things couldn't get any worse, but she is about to be proved wrong.

Disfigured by the ordeal she has somehow managed to survive, she realizes her grotesque appearance prevents her continuing her search for her mother and ends any hope of a future with Thris.

But Viv's angel blood is strong and, aided by its healing, she sets out to find the little girl. She is helped by a man whose kindness is something she has never experienced before, and love blossoms. He demands her trust, but haunted by images of witch-burnings, Viv daren't reveal what she really is. Complications multiply until being with him, and the child she loves, seems all but impossible.

Thris is bound by his pledge to guide Viv to her mother, and returns, but his search for Viv ends so catastrophically, that he yearns for death. All Viv's nightmares come true when she discovers his fate, but saving him, might cost the lives of countless others.

In Thris's absence, Ky and Ash uncover warnings about a trinity of angels the three of them resemble but who disappeared eons before in mysterious circumstances. The warnings about their fate are fragmentary, as if they have been deliberately destroyed.

Can Viv save the angel she loves? Or will she lose him and everything else she has come to care about?

If you like your female heroes feisty, your male angels glorious, your fantasy worlds filled with brilliant landscapes and a dash of romance, you will love *Angel Bound*, Book 4 in the five book fantasy series *Angel Caste*.

Buy *Angel Bound* today to continue your amazing journey with Viv and Thris through the wild worlds of the Rynth.

Book 5 Angel Blessed

It seems Lady Luck has smiled on Viv at last. Or has she?

When Viv is offered the chance of a home with the little girl she loves, she grabs it but then the child is snatched. To rescue her, not only must Viv battle the little girl's enemies, but those who love the child as well.

The perilous quest leaves Viv horribly injured, and she ends up in a world where she is offered the opportunity to finally heal herself. It means opening herself to terrible new risks but also the possibility of securing the little girl's safety, once and for all.

She returns to the child's world but is pursued by those who believe she holds the key to their deepest desires and, as their threats escalate to violence, Thris reappears. Viv's happiness soon turns to dread, as he reveals a threat that could destroy the little girl's world, as well as his own. Thris joins with Ky and Ash in a desperate fight to avoid the impending catastrophe and as events build to a climax, Viv prepares to sacrifice everything for those she loves.

Will Viv's search finally deliver her the loving home she craves? Or will she, and those she cares about, end their lives in the cataclysm that threatens?

If you like your female heroes feisty, your male angels glorious, and your fantasy worlds filled with brilliant landscapes and a dash of romance, you will love *Angel Blessed*, the final book in the five book fantasy series *Angel Caste*.

Buy *Angel Blessed* today to conclude your amazing journey with Viv and Thris through the wild worlds of the Rynth.

Angel Caste – Complete 5 Book Series

A troubled half-angel, a beautiful angel guide, a binding promise . . .

Viv is on day release from jail to attend the funeral of the thug she thinks is her father, when she comes face to face with her real father, the powerful angel Archae Kald. If finding out she's a half-angel isn't shocking enough, Viv discovers her mother isn't dead after all but lost somewhere in the tangle of worlds called the Rynth.

Determined to find the only person who has ever truly loved her, Viv goes to Kald's angel world where he appoints the beautiful Thris as her guide. Thris is kind and caring, unlike the males Viv has known before, but after living on the streets, Viv finds it almost impossible to trust.

Friendship grows as Thris trains her to travel the rifts, but the Rynth is a dark and dangerous place, even for angels and, as Thris grows increasingly tempted by Viv's emerging angel traits, disaster strikes.

Viv journeys on alone and stumbles into a war zone where she finds a lost child. She pledges to take the child to safety but, as the war rages on, deciding who is friend and who is enemy becomes a deadly game of chance.

Bound by his promise to guide Viv to her mother, Thris embarks on a desperate search for her, but a greater threat confronts them both and, in the end, they must fight not just for their own lives, but for the lives of those they love.

The Kira Chronicles - 6 book series
Book 1 The Whisper of Leaves

A gold-eyed Healer, a prophecy, two brothers at war.

In seasons long past, twin gold-eyed princes sundered a kingdom. Rejecting his brother's warrior ways, Kasheron led his people away to establish the Tremen community of Allogrenia, deep in the great southern forests. Forgotten by the outside world and protected by the trackless trees, the Tremen flourish for seasons uncounted, upholding Kasheron's legacy of peace and healing.

All Tremen delight in the healing arts, but Kira is the greatest Healer of them all.

To the north of Allogrenia, drought grips the land, and the Shargh suffer. A herding people, they lost their grazing tracts to the Northern invaders years before, through long and bloody wars. As the drought tightens its grip, and their herd animals die, the chief's younger brother seizes on an ancient prophecy to snatch the chiefship for himself.

The prophecy links the Shargh's doom to a gold-eyed Healer, and Kira has gold eyes.

The Shargh attack with devastating consequences, and Kira must fight to save the wounded. But the Shargh wounds rot, no matter her skill, and as the blood-shed continues, Kira faces losing everything and everyone she loves.

Can Kira cure the Shargh wounds? Or will the Tremen community be destroyed? If you love your female heroes feisty, your fantasy worlds with sun-dappled forests, quiet owl-filled nights, and just the right dash of romance, you will love *The Whisper of Leaves*, Book 1 of the six book *The Kira Chronicles* series.

Buy *The Whisper of Leaves* today to enter the forest world of the Tremen and start your amazing adventure with Kira as she fights to save her people.

Book 2 The Silence of Stone

How can fire quench fire?

The Tremen are dying and Kira is in a deadly race against time to save them. Somewhere deep in the Warens' labyrinth of underground tunnels, lies the answer to a riddle and the cure to Shargh wounds.

To find it, she must defeat the tunnels' unmapped darkness *and* Kest, the blue-eyed, blond-haired Commander of the Protectors. As leader of the force Kasheron established to keep the Tremen safe, Kest is sworn to protect, and everything Kira does puts her at terrible risk.

As she fights to heal, and he to protect, they join in an uneasy alliance to save the people they love.

When Kira is made Tremen Leader, the stakes rise even further. The Tremen are riven by division and Kira must fight to stop the Tremen community from breaking apart. Desperate to find the cause of the Shargh attacks and stop the Tremen's suffering, she goes ever deeper into the Warens' perilous darkness. Kest searches too, his quest in the sunlit forests above.

When he and his men make a gruesome discovery, he realizes what drives the Sharghs' murderous attacks, but then he makes a deadly mistake.

As Kira learns more of her brutal lineage, she is confronted with the horrifying truth that to save her people, she must lose them forever. Can Kira preserve Kasheron's legacy of peace and healing? Or will all he fought for be swept away by the violence he fled?

If you love your female heroes feisty, your fantasy worlds with sun-dappled forests, quiet owl-filled nights, and just the right dash of romance, you will love *The Silence of Stone*, Book 2 of the six book *The Kira Chronicles* series.

Buy *The Silence of Stone* today to enter the forest world of the Tremen and start your amazing adventure with Kira as she fights to save her people.

Book 3 The Secrets of Stars

What truths lie hidden in the stars?

Kira is alone, her food all but exhausted, the forest and those she loves, far behind her. When she stumbles on a stranger under attack, she faces a terrible choice: betray everything Kasheron fought for or walk away.

The stranger, Caledon, knows a path over the mountains and has friends nearby who can help them, but Kira's quest is clear: go straight north, gain aid for her people, and return home.

They continue together but the Azurcades are perilous and when a terrible storm threatens to sweep them to their deaths, their journey becomes a battle for survival.

Kira's trust in Caledon grows and his gentleness rouses other, deeper feelings, but Caledon is ruled by forces that pose a lethal threat to her quest. She plans her escape, but new lands bring new enemies and she is taken prisoner.

Fleeing her captors, Kira finds herself with a people under Shargh attack. As the carnage mounts and she joins with their Healers to save the wounded, her stocks of fireweed run dangerously low. Caledon strives to regain her trust and the stakes escalate when he reveals terrible truths that threaten the Tremen's very existence.

As the slaughter continues and Kira embarks on a hazardous search for fireweed, disaster strikes and she is snatched by the Shargh warrior who has long hunted her. Can Kira survive to reach the north and finally deliver aid to her people? Or will her quest end at the Shargh's brutal hands?

If you love your female heroes feisty, your fantasy worlds with sun-dappled forests, quiet owl-filled nights, and just the right dash of romance, you will love *The Secrets of Stars*, Book 3 of the six book *The Kira Chronicles* series.

Buy *The Secrets of Stars* today to enter the forest world of the Tremen and continue your amazing adventure with Kira as she fights to save her people.

Book 4 The Thunder of Hoofs

Who is friend and who is enemy?

When Kira's Shargh captors are attacked, she finds herself a prisoner of those who might prove even deadlier. But then, in a heart-rending twist of fate, their leader is revealed to be the bearer of everything Kira most loved in the world *and* everything Kasheron most despised.

Kira hides her identity but her subterfuge is discovered and the dangers multiply. Her quest is to gain aid from her northern kin, but the forests that hid the Tremen from enemies, also hid them from friends, and there is no help for a people without alliance or treaty. To make matters worse, the northern histories tell a very different story of the great Healer Kasheron.

To aid the Tremen, Kira must turn south again, to where Caledon will bring the Tremen fighters but she and the northern leader share a powerful attraction and he's determined to keep her safely in the north, far from the Shargh.

Desperate to learn of Kira's fate, Caledon journeys north too and they are reunited, but his arrival generates antagonisms that threaten alliances and treaties alike. As Caledon strives to decipher the stars' intent, the stakes escalate, and he fears following his heart could cause the deaths of countless others.

Kira is no slave to the stars and, driven by her duties as leader, sets out for the south. Besieged by squalling winds and icy storms, her escort comes under Shargh attack and she finds herself in a desperate flight through the night in a terrifying attempt to outrun them. But Shargh hunters lie in wait, and in a deadly rain of spears, her mare goes down. Can Kira survive to finally deliver aid to her people? Or will her quest end in the wind-swept darkness?

If you love your female heroes feisty, your fantasy worlds with sun-dappled forests, quiet owl-filled nights, and just the right dash of romance, you will love *The Thunder of Hoofs*, Book 4 of the six book *The Kira Chronicles* series.

Buy *The Thunder of Hoofs* today to enter the forest world of the Tremen and continue your amazing adventure with Kira as she fights to save her people.

Book 5 The Crying of Birds

Must Tremen healing bow before Terak swords?

Kira's deepest fears are realized when the Tremen are forced from the forests to join the devastating conflict on the plain. To add to her guilt, she can't remain with the people she leads but must go north. Sarnia has no healing, and if the fighting spreads, their wounded will die.

Leaving behind those she loves, she endures the perilous journey back to Sarnia, only to confront powerful forces determined to keep the ways of the despised Healer Kasheron out of the city. As Kira fights to create a place of healing, aid comes from an unexpected quarter, but a healing place without fireweed will save no lives.

Kira's search for fireweed grows increasingly desperate and then her worst nightmare comes true when the person she loves most in the world is mortally wounded. As the fighting drags on and winter deepens, the injured flood in and Kira's struggle to save them takes a deadly toll.

In the south, the Shargh tribes join, and Tierken makes a terrible mistake that puts Sarnia at risk. Distrust weakens their forces and as the bloodshed grows, treachery promises to deliver a Shargh victory. And then, as Tierken and his men fight for their very existence, word reaches him that Kira's life hangs in the balance. Faced with a terrible dilemma, he makes a choice that risks the destruction of his leadership in the north

Kira flees to the healing settlement of Kessom but to reach its sanctuary, she must navigate the raging torrent that claimed

Tierken's father. Will Kira survive to reach the healing she so desperately needs? Or will her journey end in the watery darkness?

If you love your female heroes feisty, your fantasy worlds with sun-dappled forests, quiet owl-filled nights, and just the right dash of romance, you will love *The Crying of Birds*, Book 5 of the six book *The Kira Chronicles* series.

Buy *The Crying of Birds* today to enter the forest world of the Tremen and continue your amazing adventure with Kira as she fights to save her people.

Book 6 The Music of Home

What is the price of peace?

With the fighting over, Tierken pursues Kira to Kessom where she is overjoyed to be reunited with him, but neither have escaped the battles unscathed. Kira's health is fragile and Tierken's aggression is honed from months of fighting. To add to the complications, Tierken's enemies in Sarnia have taken full advantage of his absence in the south.

Angered by their scheming and frustrated by Kira's refusal to bend to his will, his arguments with her escalate until Kira realizes the breach between the Tremen and Terak is too large for her to mend. Her hopes for a future with Tierken shattered, she sets out for home, but the Sarsalin is full of dangers and enemies lie in wait.

Caledon waits too as he struggles to reconcile his own want of Kira with the wants and needs of the stars. They travel south together and when they come upon a sick Shargh child, Kira begins to understand the brutal consequences of the fighting, and that bloodshed can only ever seed more bloodshed.

Desperate to prevent future warfare, Kira resolves to offer the Shargh people healing, despite knowing it will likely cost her life. But when she reaches the Shargh settlement, she makes a shocking discovery that changes everything.

There are Shargh women there who crave peace as she does, but she comes face to face with the man who believes her death will deliver him everything he desires, and as the final chilling part of the last Telling unfolds, she realizes for the first time, what is truly precious to her and what is worth fighting for.

Will Kira survive to return to all she loves, or make the ultimate sacrifice as she strives for peace?

If you love your female heroes feisty, your fantasy worlds with sun-dappled forests, quiet owl-filled nights, and just the right dash of romance, you will love *The Music of Home*, the final installment in *The Kira Chronicles* series.

Buy *The Music of Home* today to enter the forest world of the Tremen and complete your amazing adventure with Kira as she fights to save her people.

The Kira Chronicles – Complete 6 Book Series

A gold-eyed Healer, a prophecy, two brothers at war.

In seasons long past, twin gold-eyed princes sundered a kingdom. Rejecting his brother Terak's warrior ways, Kasheron led his people deep into the great southern forests and established the healing settlement of Allogrenia. The Tremen flourished, upholding Kasheron's legacy of peace and healing, and protected by the vast, trackless trees.

All Tremen delight in the healing arts, but Kira is the greatest Healer of them all.

To the north of Allogrenia, drought ravages the Shargh's land, and as their suffering escalates, the chief's younger brother seizes on an ancient prophecy to snatch the chiefship for himself. The prophecy links the Shargh's doom to a gold-eyed Healer, and Kira has gold eyes.

The Shargh attack with devastating consequences and Kira must fight to save the wounded, but the Shargh wounds rot, no matter her skill, and Kira finds herself in a deadly race against time. As the slaughter continues, she makes the horrifying discovery that the Shargh hunt *her*. To halt the attacks and save her people, she sets off for the North to seek aid from her long sundered warrior kin.

But the dangers beyond the forests exceed even the Shargh attacks. The Tremen detest their warrior kin but Terak's descendants have inflicted a worse fate on the Tremen. Kira's new-found love is torn apart by ancient hostilities and when trust turns to betrayal, it risks everything she has fought for.

135

As the battles rage on, Kira becomes increasingly sickened by the bloodshed. Desperate to end the suffering once and for all, she sets out on a quest that could cost her everything and everyone she loves.

Fantasy Novels

The Emerald Serpent

Check out the fabulous book trailer:

https://www.youtube.com/watch?v=bGpKxnpCEMg

Betrayal, torture, death: Etaine lives on only to destroy those who robbed her of everything she loved.

Seven years before, Etaine met fellow Ranger Cormac, the he-Eadar she believed was her longed-for true-mate. Emerald-eyed, white-skinned, and black-haired, the Eadar had formed into Ranger bands to fight the Fada, invading religious zealots determined to replace the Eadar's Serpent Goddess with their own gods of stone.

The pure blood of the ancient Eadar runs strong in Etaine and Cormac's veins, and their joining had the potential to open the Emerald and Serpent Ways to them, old worlds only true Eadar can enter. But their love affair goes tragically amiss, with catastrophic consequences.

Etaine flees and as the years pass, slowly rebuilds her life, but the Fada's attacks grow more ferocious, and the Eadar are forced to fight for their very existence. When the Fada mass to commit yet more bloody slaughter, and the bands join in a final, desperate effort to defeat them, Etaine comes under Cormac's command, the very last Eadar she ever wants to see again.

Together they have a weapon that can destroy the Fada, but to use it, Etaine must learn to trust again and Cormac to Remember. And time runs short: the Serpent rises.

137

Don't miss the enthralling story of Etaine and Cormac's fight to defeat the Fada and revive the old worlds of the Eadar. Set in the ancient Caledonian Forest of Northern Scotland, with its misty crags and bright, rushing streams, *The Emerald Serpent* will delight those who love their fantasy with a touch of Celtic and a dash of romance.

Buy *The Emerald Serpent* today to share Etaine and Cormac's amazing quest to rid their beautiful worlds of the Fada threat.

Heart Hunter

Fleet is a young Sceadu hunter: skilled, strong, and fast. She hunts deep into the icy mountains, seeking meat for her people, for the rains have failed and plunged the Sceaudu into hunger.

Her hunts are hard, but she has much to look forward to. Soon she will be gifted her air-name by the Sceadu's shaman, and then she will be a full adult, and free to marry the man she loves.

But while Fleet is on hunt, the old shaman dies, and the new shaman visions a very different future for her: cross the frozen, ice-locked mountains and complete a perilous quest or lose the man she loves forever.

In a moment of anger and frustration, Fleet commits a terrible wrong and sets out into the frigid mountains to atone with her life. In a journey that takes her deep into the earth's darkest places, into strange new worlds, and even into Death itself, she discovers that only she can save her people. To survive, she must draw on every shred of her hunter strength, and doing the impossible, it turns out, is just the beginning.

If you love strong, independent female hunters, bright snowy landscapes, worlds where truth might lie in the mystical realms of a vision-quest, and a dash of romance, you will love *Heart Hunter*.

Buy *Heart Hunter* today to share Fleet's danger, joy, and discoveries in her quest to save her people and the man she loves.

The Third Moon

Where does the past end and the future begin?

Haunted by inherited memories of his people's dispossession and theft of their children, Warrain is just twelve years old when the nightmare repeats. But Warrain isn't living on Earth in the 21st Century, he is living on the planet Imago in the far flung future.

Five years before, Station One's Mech's got high on the opioid arrash, and in the bloodshed that followed, Warrain's scientific community were expelled from the Station, his father murdered, and his mother and unborn sibling lost to him.

The scientists carve out a rudimentary Station high in Imago's ranges, and Warrain's friends get on with their lives. Not Warrain; he climbs the Tors to stare down at Station One, dream of his mother and sibling, and plot revenge.

And then one day, everything changes. A third moon appears in the sky, one of Imago's life-forms calls him by name, and disease breaks out at Station One.

When the Mechs visit to seek help for their ill, Warrain seizes the opportunity to deal them a blow they will never forget. But the third moon brings changes that threaten them all and, to aid the life-form whose kind is being dispossessed and slaughtered, he must turn his back on the hate that has long sustained him and find another way to live.

If you are fascinated by the power of memory, the excitement of life on other planets, and like your fantasy with a dash of romance, you will love *The Third Moon*.

Buy *The Third Moon* today to share Warrain's life on Imago as he struggles to protect Imago's creatures and make the planet truly his home.

Messenger

In a world made deaf by hatred, who will hear the messenger?

Severine's world ends the day her family is murdered. Being raised in the loving community of gay Travelers always marked her as an outsider, but being female puts her in mortal danger. Women are scarce, precious, and hunted.

When chance brings Severine face to face with the father she has never known, he assigns the son of his murdered best friend to guard her. They soon clash. Severine believes all men are violent brutes and Jeph resents his freedoms being curtailed.

An uneasy understanding grows but Jeph is glad to deliver her to the Enclaves, a sanctuary her father has carved out in the mountains for his women and children. But there is no safety in a world broken by war and sickness and when violence follows her, Severine flees to the northern city of Andhaka in search of a home amongst her mother's people. Jeph follows, bound by loyalty to her father, but the north holds terrible dangers for him.

It's been years since Andhaka has welcomed outsiders with anything but bullets, and to survive and to protect Jeph, Severine must learn to use her enemies' weapons against them. As the stakes rise, she comes to understand the horror of her mother's loss, and what drove her father north seventeen years before. His quest becomes her quest, but she hasn't counted on the savage legacy that war and sickness have left behind, or on falling in love.

142

Can Severine succeed where her father failed? Or will her fate prove even deadlier than his? If you love your fantasy set in brilliant new worlds, with characters you really care about, and just the right dash of romance, you will love *Messenger*.

Buy *Messenger* today to share Severine's journey as she fights for a home, the man she loves, and a better world.

I Heard the Wolf Call My Name *Finalist Best YA Novel –*
2019 Aurealis Awards

Jax is on the run from his past. A shifter from the island of
Rua, he is trapped on the mainland amongst the despised
Off-islanders. Even worse, he is in the military, with a less
than exemplary military record.

So when he is ordered to pack up his kit and is flown away
in the middle of the night, he is in no position to argue. And
it isn't as if he has any other place to go.

Ten years before, when Jax was just twelve years old and in
bird-form high above his island home, it blew to smithereens,
leaving him the only survivor, or so he believes.

The mystery flight dumps him at a new base where he comes
face to face with Matiu, the boyhood friend Jax thought was
as dead as his previous life. The military want Jax for an
important mission and Matiu wants Jax too, but for different
reasons, but there is no way Jax is going to resurrect what
took him ten long years to bury.

As the pressure on him ramps up, Jax flees but is confronted
by something more deadly than his nightmarish memories.
To stop the other Islanders suffering the same fate as his
people, Jax must finally face who and what he really is and
decide where he truly belongs.

Like stories that question what it means to be human? That
escape the narrow definitions of friendship and love? If so,
you will enjoy Jax and Anahera's journeys.

Buy *I Heard the Wolf Call My Name* to see the world through
very different eyes.

The Dragon of the Drowned World (Young Adult)

When the earth shivers and shakes and the oceans rise over the lands, thirteen year old Jojo washes up on a strange shore. The adult survivors build a ramshackle settlement from the debris the ocean delivers, and make sense of their predicament by comparing themselves to Noah and his Ark.

But not everyone agrees and all Jojo wants is his family back.

He scours the beach each day looking for things that aren't broken or dirty and stumbles on a strange, silvery plate. When the plate is smashed by an older boy, Jojo stores the pieces in his secret cave, but then odd things start to happen. The ferocious blood crabs give way to him on the beach and when he's attacked by a giant serpent, it suddenly lets him go.

His fellow wash up, Lee, finds a strange, poisoned little creature and friendship grows as they team up to save it. Lee insists the creature is a griffin and Jojo's plate pieces belong to a loong or dragon but Jojo has enough problems without adding mythic creatures to the list.

When Lee's little creature takes to the skies and the adults set out to hunt it down, Jojo and Lee embark on a desperate quest to save it. But as their journey takes them ever deeper into danger and the plates seem to grow in power, Jojo fears the dragon might turn out to be the deadliest creature of them all.

Like adventure stories where mythic animals come alive? Where characters tackle the really big questions about life? You'll love *The Dragon of the Drowned World*.

www.ingramcontent.com/pod-product-compliance
Lightning Source LLC
Chambersburg PA
CBHW070332130626
46556CB00007B/2820